A Shadow Before Me

Lanayre Liggera

A Shadow Before Me

Copyright © 2021 by Lanayre Liggera. All rights reserved.

Additional Copies:

www.amazon.com
www.barnesandnoble.com

Published in the United States of America

ISBN Paperback: *9781956895209*

Now, Carter's experience with Mercy had been idyllic: but, living in a neighborhood, he had been forced to realize that children always prefer the biggest backyard in the neighborhood, so, because they had the biggest back yard—hardly an estate, but a few portions more of grass—Mercy's companions somehow always ended up there, boys and girls alike, with high pitched voices, screams, giggles, laughter.

Annoying as it was to Carter, he kept reminding himself that he was rather old to be a father; he bought a radio with headphones.

Seeing Valerie look into his office one night while he was listening to music as he wrote up trial notes, he attempted to give her a cheery wave.

"Carter," she asked her spouse, "What do you think if we set a time for Mercy to come inside for dinner and homework. When you get home, go out the back door to greet her as a signal for her to come inside, and her friends will go home."

Mercy seemed at ease with her mother's suggestion that when Poppy came home, family time would commence. It took a bit of a prodding the first week, but Carter's arrival, with his car and driver, which caused a run to the front fence to watch, was an excellent sign that the sands of time had run out for the day. Then, the two of them leaned against the fence for a few minutes watching the children straggle home.

"That girl moves so slowly, sometimes I think she would rather sleep on the sidewalk."

Daddy," said Mercy earnestly "She hasn't got any dinner to come home to." She did not realize she had not called him 'Poppy', so engrossed was she in this childhood problem which cried out for adult wisdom. But as she uttered the word Daddy, Carter felt a sensation as if Adrian had tapped him on his shoulder, and asked, "Does justice only happen in court?"

"And why is that?"

"Her Mommy drinks."

There you are, Judge. You've forgotten what it was like have problems as a child. It was not that Carter was unused to dead drunk parents—in his early innocence, he felt it only occurred in neighborhoods like his, but in visits to country houses he had seen people so drunk they could not get out of their chairs, women so drunk they vomited on their clothing.

When he entered the house, he asked his wife to put another plate on. "Mercy tells me we have a little neighborhood problem. I'm off to look into it—I shan't be long."

Having taken off his suit jacket and necktie, he substituted a sporting jacket thrown over his shoulders and trainers as if he were out for a jog; neighbors were familiar with his exercising down the block. Sometimes there was a hello, or a wave, which he was happy to return.

No wig or red robe this time, judge. He was so worked up he rang the doorbell and knocked on the door at the same time. The door opened to reveal a dishevelled woman leaning against the door jamb.

"Who are you?" The demand was slurred, aggressive.

"Your neighbor who lives at the end of the block. I have come to invite your daughter to dinner with our daughter Mercy tonight."

"How bloody nice. Tomorrow night too, is that the idea?"

"Yes, that is the idea. We shall invite her until you can provide her with an evening meal. It would be the least obvious method of dealing with the situation."

"Oh, you will, will you, Mister la-di-da Busybody? She can't do that without my permission."

"Quite the opposite. I am a judge, and there are laws in England dealing with childhood negligence which would take a dim view of your inability to feed her a proper supper. This would be the easiest and most neighborly way to deal with this situation without creating undue interference."

"Yeah, is that so?"

"If there is no improvement in this situation, the court can remove her from your home, Madame. And I warn you if there is any bruise on this child tomorrow after this conversation, I shall pursue these charges to the full extent of the law."

"Yeah? Well, here's my answer!"

Breaking her whisky bottle against the door jamb, she came at him with the ragged glass edges; in an instant, Carter recalled Khalil's technique.

The woman expected he would back away; instead, he abruptly stepped forward. She took a swing at him, which cut through the fabric of his jacket and shirt into his neck, where he felt the warmth of starting to bleed, but he did not begin to feel it was a bleed-to-death cut. So, instead of what she expected, he stepped *forward,* grasping her forearm, twisting it firmly behind her.

"Ouch!" she screamed.

"Drop the bottle." He pushed into the house, with her stepping backwards lest her arm be twisted more. She dropped the bottle. "Step in back of your daughter. I am going to report this, but only for the record; there will be no trial for aggravated assault. I can assure you going to court is not a pleasant experience, so I am allowing some time to get sober enough for you to consider your options. Come, Jane," he said to the terrified little girl, holding out a hand while keeping her mother's arm still gripped by the other hand. "Let's go up to our house for dinner." Still holding her hand in one hand, he held his jacket against his neck with the other to staunch the bleeding.

"Well," said Valerie, as she opened the door to find a blood-stained husband holding hands with a little girl. "You never know what you will find when you open the door! Someone needs stitches!" *Wives…they are over protective…but don't forget, it is because she loves you.*

"Put on a good dressing then I shall call Jack."

"Who is…?"

"The court physician." He had seen him just this afternoon as he passed by the fencing room, where he was subjected to the usual repartee about why he didn't learn a real sport, all he used was one finger.

Jack Dalton came by shortly after dinner. Carter had lain down on the kitchen floor, not wanting to drag blood into any carpeted room. He was still holding his jacket against the cut.

Valerie had thrown a sheet over the kitchen table, so she and Jack lifted Carter onto it.

"Nasty. Luckily she missed your ceratoid artery—you were right to call me. Local anaesthetic," he explained to Mercy, who was, indubitably, on the pale side, as the needle went into her Poppy's neck. "Let me know when it takes hold."

"All right," said Carter. Jack began to probe the neck wound after removing Valerie's dressing. "Mmmm. Good idea you rang me. There are small bits of fabric and glass in here. Hold still." He placed them carefully on a piece of gauze. "Here you go, young lady. Keep them. Good evidence if needed," he said to Mercy.

Mercy returned as Carter flinched slightly on the first stitch. "Here, Poppy, take my hand!"

When he was finished, Jack advised Carter to lie still for half an hour to recuperate. Then he went up to bed, but could not find a comfortable way to lie with stitches in his neck, so, for fear his restlessness would wake Valerie, he decided to go next room over. As he started to slide out of bed a remarkably strong hand on his elbow stopped him.

"Don't move anywhere. That would make me worry."

CHAPTER 1

They had found their house one day when they were walking in Regent's Park, then wandering up and down on streets near the water in Maida Vale. On the London side of the bridge, several streets back from the Grand Canal, stood a house marked "for sale," built of now -weathered yellow brick peeking through white wash, a tile roof with topped with castings, fronted by rusted collapsing railing with stumps of what might have once been a boxwood hedge.

"Isn't that charming?"

Oh yes here we go. She definitely will have to wrestle with that hedge!

They had rented a small house after moving out of Carter's flat. It stood in a mews, below the lawn surfaces, where it seemed protective and private; but as time went on, as Carter put it, they began to feel more and more safe housed, and had begun to look for something else.

Now, without any further words, he said, "I'll call the agent on my mobile." Oddly, she appeared ready to drop everything to speed out to the house, instead of making a future appointment. When she opened the door, its prospective owners could see why.

Inside, rain had taken its toll on a swathe of wood on the second floor, where the walls had been so warped by the rain which had managed to trickle down behind it from the gutters, it would have to be replaced. Carter whispered in his wife's ear, "Don't glow!" He knew she was already seeing what Adry could do for this house, assessing whether it had good 'bones.'

Carter could see why the agent had hurried; this house, she assessed, would be as old as Methuselah without selling. Was she willing to drop the price? Was she ever! This property would need major renovation. He was negotiating with her in one room while Valerie was moving around, and she cried, "Oh! Here is an old Aga cooker in the kitchen! Four ovens!"

Is that what that monster is called. Whatever its color is, I can at least tell that it is an intense one.

Valerie immediately called her son to ask if he could look the inside of the house over, then draw her up an appraisal. Oh, yes, they would come that weekend!

He wrote up a list of all that needed fixing and the approximate costs to present to the realtor. Carter was somehow sure if the Sidi were here, he could haggle her into an even lower price, but the one figure she descended to was low enough for them. Now it was time for tea. Fortunately the realtor had left an electric teapot, a box of fresh tea, a strainer, and half a dozen cups and saucers as well as a milk jug and sugar packets.

Suddenly, Adry changed topic. "Mum, we have an announcement," he said, as Valerie set down the tea tray.

"You're not!' she exclaimed.

"We are."

Oh…*my little boy is all grown up.* "Carter! You are going to become a grandfather!"

"Adry-have –have-they a manual on it?" Carter stuttered. For once in his life, he was caught absolutely flat-footed.

"I don't think so," Brie chimed in. "Just tons of books about *good* parenting! None of them agree with one another."

"Here's a copy of the estimate I made for the realtor." She whistled. "Of course, I would give you a discount!"

"Not on your life!"

They had not put their first home lease on the market until the yellow house was fit to inhabit. Security was not thrilled with their location, and installed bolt locks, alarmed the windows— which were made of shatterproof glass—and installed special locks on them that were used for the owners of firearms if they went out, as well as mounting louvered shutters inside the windows which could swing open during the day, and closed and locked at night.

Ah my dear wife; for us there is not a thin line between good and evil but a roundabout.

Carter had imagined dripping sentiment; but his wife just moved the furniture and the chandelier, ready to start all over. What was it Adry had told him? Falconers renovate until they die.

CHAPTER 2

After their first return to England, after his three years of safe-housing, which was finally ended in Texas, as well as the rather inconceivable notion that he had married, when they stepped inside, Carter noticed the red light blinking frantically for voice mail. "How many?" he asked Pan.

"Forty-six. All reporters!"

Carter had pushed the 'delete' button.

Nevertheless, Carter had been interviewed to death upon their first return anyway. Many reporters pounced on him, cleverly trying the elicit something he had not meant to say, to procure a 'scoop,' which would compromise intelligence.

And what would I have told them, that a song they sang at the ranch with the lyric, 'love's the greatest healer to be found,' was the biggest happening.

Carter learned to say, "No comment." After a journey on which ostentatiously nothing noteworthy had happened, no reporters were hovering at Heathrow or Gatwick.

The evening, however, brought one lone inquiring call from Mildred Stevenson of the *Times*, who, after ringing Heathrow and Gatwick, tried private airstrips like Farnborough, where she found an informant who affirmed a landing of one of Sidi's aircraft at 4:24 that afternoon, and when asked for his name, was happy to give it, as Miss Stevenson explained that her newspaper prided itself on accuracy.

This time home, upstairs, opening suitcases, dirty laundry in the wash. A surprise awaited; Mercy had learned how to use the microwave, so they sat down for dinner. Chicken!

She rang that evening. He arranged to meet her at his office the next morning, and asked Valerie to make a call to his clerk to that effect.

CHAPTER 3

On the way out the door that morning, Carter noted a piece of paper held down by a rock. Over their years together, he had learned a great, great deal from his wife. He picked it up and identified it as a hex symbol, then stuffed it into his inside pocket.

His secretary, Miss Penelope Thomas, otherwise known as simply MsT., buzzed him to announce that Miss Stevenson was here.

"Have her come through, MsT."

The door opened, and the usual formalities followed: "His honor." "Miss Mildred Stevenson." This followed by a brief handshake.

"Would you care for tea?" They both indicated not.

His secretary helped her doff her coat, hanging it up next to his winter and summer red robes. His winter robe, replete with white fur, always made him feel like Santa Claus. The black jacket and waistcoat he wore as to ascertain what evidence was available for a potential trial was far more sober.

She was an older woman who still wore hats, secured with lovely hat pins, while the hair beneath was untouched grey, held in place by a barely visible hairnet.

She dressed impeccably, elegantly; her suit was subdued but expensive tweed, her shoes, likewise, of softest leather, a perfect match for her suit, which was predominantly brown. Little of her clothing was new; she had bought very well from items meant to last a lifetime. She wore no makeup save for lipstick and powder, as well as gloves, not, he knew, particularly for style, but to protect her from germs, for she never knew where her work would take her. Now, she removed them, putting them in her pocket book which she closed with a snap.

In her way, he thought, she had echoes of Claudia, except that her outfits were always inconspicuous, so as not to draw attention to herself, but direct the limelight to the person she was interviewing.

"Miss Stevenson, would you care to sit on the sofa, or prefer an armchair?"

"Lovely." She picked the sofa; she never crossed her legs, but put both feet on the ground. Once she had crossed them at the ankles when she had a knee injury.

"Well, Sir Carter, since last we met, a great deal has happened. How do you feel about your safehousing now, in retrospect, if you do not mind me asking?"

"Preferable to being dead." He smiled as he said it.

"Mm mm. You were under government protection then, were you not? MI6?"

"Yes, they arranged everything." She sensed a non-full-disclosure the way some people instantly smell Chanel No. 5. Swiftly, she changed topics, so she could take time, then circle around again.

"Your marriage was quite a surprise! Valerie Falconer, the one who creates those funny little stickers!"

You'd be surprised how much money those funny little stickers bring in, Miss Stevenson! But aloud he replied, "Quite a surprise for me as well, Miss Stevenson!"

"Is that her photograph on your desk?"

"No, that is Mercy, my god daughter. She's going ten now. As for my wife, I had known her for some time. She was married to my best friend, then widowed after he had a stroke. We were quite aware of each other's foibles when we made the decision." He reached for his brief. "I was going to take these photographs to be framed today."

One was a Valerie at full tilt on a black Arabian horse, hair streaming out from beneath a checkered head dress held in place with a black band; in the other, she was seated on a dapple grey, with a great smile, for the horse was fully decorated with the Royal Cavalry of Oman silver trappings.

My Valerie.

"What did your wife think of your safe housing?"

"You know as well as I do, Miss Stevenson, she knew as little as possible. As is designed to be the case, the object is to keep one's friends out of harm's way. Her family home is in the Forest of Dean, and, as well, she herself was undergoing great personal and financial difficulties."

"You were married before?"

"Very briefly."

"You get on with your wife's other children?"

"Oh, yes. You see, the other two are older—I've known them since they were children."

"May I ask why you visited Jordan in particular?"

"To visit an old friend."

Then something completely unexpected happened. She had *not* circled around as he anticipated; she came straight on.

"Sir Carter, here is a photo from our reporter from Cairo." She put the photo on his desk. There he was, with Valerie next to him, about five feet to one side of the Sidi, who was addressing the people.

There goes our cover….

"The photograph was taken after an alleged miracle," he explained. "It happened under the under the ecclesiastical jurisprudence of the Coptic Orthodox church. And as I am sure you know, it will undergo a rigorous examination under Coptic law, which is just as complex as secular law! But it has also been approved as a miracle by the Vatican.

"Our host had taken us to Zeitoun, where an apparition—I think that is the correct term—of what Christians believe to be the Virgin Mary had appeared over a local church during a period of three years when he was a young man. He had visited the site many times, collecting as series of photographs, year by year."

"My head is spinning slightly," said Miss Henderson. "I am glad I have a tape recorder! You were among the party accompanying this man in Egypt?"

"We were. His legs had been paralyzed."

"Can we speak off-record for a sentence or two?" She turned off her tape recorder. "I am what you might call a spiritual late bloomer, Miss Stevenson." She turned the recorder back on.

"Our reporter was unable to catch what was said on a tape recorder, but some people informed him the man's name was the Sidi el Hassem, of almost legendary reputation, also that he used a phrase, 'The children of Abraham.'"

"Yes, you see this apparition was seen by Christians, Muslims and Jews, the so-called Abrahamic covenant. The photograph was taken when the police were summoned to move the crowd back to the edge of the stairs."

"Remarkable, remarkable! Tell me, are you giving this story to other reporters, milord?"

"No, Miss Stevenson, it is yours, and yours alone. I made that decision as over the years I have found you to be truthful and accurate without gilding the lily. I know you have no control over the release of the photograph by the *Times*."

"You know," she said, "there will be a storm of debate over the idea of a miracle."

"I have already requested an unlisted phone number. Tell me, Miss Stevenson, what do *you* think of miracles?"

"I am—a believer, Sir Carter. I read C. S Lewis's book on miracles though it was a bit heavy going on natural law to me. If I may comment, this is really too complex for newspaper articles. You should write a book."

"Me?"

"Why not?" Her hand was on his elbow, in the old, traditional, elegant manner as they exited the office.

"But I'd need one of those—agents or whatever."

'I'd be available! Believe me, it would fly off the shelves!"

"Interesting lady!" said MsT., a name Carter had devised for her. (She was quite proud of her nickname).

All during those long three years she had been at her desk early, too anxious to wait to see if he were all right. A little morning chat—sports, news movies—brought him back into the human sphere again. In short, Carter would not have traded her for the Tower of London.

After he had seen Miss Stevenson into a cab, he turned to his office, to begin to vest for a hearing upcoming this afternoon, when MsT. buzzed him.

C H A P T E R   4

"Sir Carter, we've received an important looking envelope delivered by courier."

"Bring it through," he said.

It was from a man at MI6 he had met during the oil bunkering affair. 'Could you slip in for a meet this p.m.? Ewen,' it read.

But below it was just the initial C' in green ink, the traditional insignia of the head of MI6 since the days of Maxwell Cummings, its first chief. Naturally, with the British proclivity for tradition, it had become one.

"Damn, a postponement!" He muttered. "MsT., please call my driver."

MI6 was a massive building, constructed of beige stone inter-mixed with portions of green glass, seated by the Thames, fronted by a small park with well-trimmed trees. None the less, it breathed forth an aura of menace, and the first time he entered the building, he was strangely afflicted by the fear he might never come out again. After his driver left him off, he was guided by a man who led him through a byzantine maze of hallways, yet he suspected he would end in Ewen MacGregor's office.

They had met several times during the oil bunker case. Mac-Gregor had annoyed him by making the same joke over and again, since he was bald, perhaps Carter could loan him some hair? Because he was a bit overly sensitive today, Carter now noticed how these little stupidities gave one a sense of reality. Sure enough, a man in a grey striped suit stood up, hand extended. "Carter, my boy! Jolly glad to see you! What the blazes were you doing in Jordan?"

"Visiting the Sidi."

"How is the old chap? We've had minimal contact with him—we heard he was wandering about the desert preaching."

"Unfortunately, an accident had put him *hors de combat*. He had to walk with crutches, as a rock hit him in the lower spine rendering him a paraplegic."

"Past tense?"

"Yes. You'll find it in the news. But, Ewen, there was a green 'C' at the bottom of your letter!"

"There is something I'd like to run through you, Carter, or I would not have pulled you out of chambers."

"What, pray tell?"

"I suspect it is one of those pesky household chores but one must always follow up to keep up cordial relations. The Sidi always sends a courier when people have visited him, with copies of their stamped passports. We have not received any dealing with your visit."

"You mean that the courier has gone missing? Have you sent out any scouts?"

"Yes, however, they've come up empty."

"Have you notified the Sidi? He has better trackers than yours."

"We hesitate to do that—it would be a loss of face for us! Gossip is some of the younger agents have it in for the Sidi because his resources are better than ours."

He knows they have run out of time for Sidi to send an acknowledgement of the reception of the paperwork the Sidi sends to MI6. But he can't say anything because he is MI6. It needs a third party. Me. No wonder he thought the matter was urgent.

"There's another question I have for you, Carter. United States intelligence has gifted us with a location in North Vietnam to which various intelligence sources communicate. But some odd bits of disinformation have been appearing lately. Would you know anything about it?"

"Is the information on the intake, or only the outgoing memo?"

"Both."

Brother-in-law George must have found a way to leak this intelligence to a United States source without giving away his location. I'm not going to tell Ewen that George's boys have turned informant on their grandmother.

CHAPTER 5

While Carter was going flat out that first day, with no time to brood or contemplate, Valerie was having a bout of the 'day at home alone visitations' which had plagued her since they had first moved to their renovated house.

She attempted to discipline herself to pray or read the Bible with no success. Old memories came flooding through her head, from days gone by, when she had lived in the country of Texas or Forest of Dean, or even visited the Sidi. She had always been involved in whatever business she was living with—ranching, foresting.

Today, she tried not to think about Adrian, without success, of course. She was nineteen years old, on a family trip to London, walking in the National Art Gallery, stopping to stare intently at a portrait of General Chinese Gordon in his Royal Engineers uniform. *Could anyone's eyes really have ever been that blue?*

Someone stopping beside her: a male voice: "They say his eyes could see right through you." It was Adrian.

Now that was more than a lifetime away and she was in a middle-aged marriage. There would be no children; she nearing the age of menopause. Instead there would be grandchildren.

She had always been involved in whatever business she was living with—ranching, foresting.

One day when she went to his chambers to meet him, the impact of all the books on the shelves in his chamber and home office suddenly struck her. She was married to a judge, who also was a public figure. What could he have seen in her?

She had always been nonchalantly deprecatory about his profession in the past, for there was no reason to take it seriously; she was living in another world. He was just a friend who came to visit.

Now, there had been hurdles to clear: dinner parties or social events at Carter's official London residence, with a staff including a butler. They were to plunge into this together, for he was forbidden such events during his safehouseing as a security risk.

"My decadent period has but one thing to recommend it—I know which bloody fork to use!" was his comment. "They may suspect what we might serve for dinner?"

"I could ask Pop to have it flash frozen and flown in. You don't think it's too commercial?"

"The High Court is a palace of conspicuous consumption, sweetheart."

"Good. Because when it comes to the family business I am an unabashed shark. What about some bourbon?"

She realized these occasions would be full of shop talk she did not understand; once in a while she would have an individual conversation about something else. She listened for phrases she would later ask Carter about, such as, "What is this C.P.S.?" However, in general, she felt like a potted plant sitting on the windowsill. But there was excitement in the kitchen when a box of frozen Herrington Beef arrived, packed with dry ice: it was followed by a package from brother George, containing bourbon, tequila and triple sec for Margueritas.

Valerie found a large set of place holders in a vintage store, bought them, and painted each place card. "You'll have to arrange them, I haven't a clue," she said to her spouse, who was so touched by this little attention to detail, he kissed her.

Perhaps this will turn out to be a bit of all right. And it almost did, except for one female date who chose their dinner as a platform to announce she did not eat meat. Valerie drilled into her eyes to ask, "And just what did you expect to be served at a formal dinner?"

Carter had cringed but righted himself and asked the butler to ring down to the dining room kitchen for a vegetarian plate. It arrived while everyone else had gone on to dessert, into which her companion tucked in as vigorously as he had the rest of the meal. *I'll wager he never asks her out again.*

Then, there were possible spells out of London at Circuit Court Duty; as to these, Carter had registered he would prefer as little of these as possible, due to family obligations. Most judges, he told her, were too old *to* have a family obligation like theirs! After three years hiding, no one really dared ask Carter to go out of town

Last, there were 'sittings'—the four traditional periods of the year when High Court operated: Michaelmas, Hilary, Easter, and Trinity, all neatly marked off on Carter's calendar.

O, she had a temper; but Adrian could calculate the moment when steam was about to issue from her ears and say, "Come on, Red, let's walk it out.

Carter was confrontational. It is what he did for a living. Confronted with a refutation, she realized her temper was not at all under control, as she had thought. What had they told Sidi? They were trying not to get mad at the same time. It had happened— once.

They were seated at the kitchen table with their checkbooks. Carter had a calculator. Valerie just ran an eye down the amounts and signed the total.

"Don't you check it?"

"No, Pop always said it would come out even in the end."

"You've never been poor!"

"Am I supposed to apologize for that? Take your three years without paying a shilling for living in the lap of luxury, and maybe it will *all* even out! What do you want me to do?" She threw out her arms in exasperation.

"Nothing. Nothing. All I've managed to acquire is a bloody headache," he had said.

"That's the thing about me I hate—my temper."

What about Jesus? Did he ever get angry? Of course he did, but always for the right reasons, it seems, if you exclude frustration and exasperation at the disciples for being so thick. I guess that was his human part. That makes me a little sad for the disciples because people used to think I was thick.

But her new husband had surprised her. "What did Adrian do when you were angry?"

"He walked it out with me."

Valerie knew that look on his face: it was one of his occasional brainstorms.

"I've got a better idea. Come with me."

They got into the Rover and he had backed out. He drove a few miles to a local hotel. After he stopped, he opened her door for her.

The clerk looked up and they could both see what he thought—a couple with no luggage. He could infer what they were up to!

Carter signed the register with his middle name, Edmond, then slid the book to her. "Sign up in whatever persona you are today!" he said, with a half-smile.

She looked at his signature, then wrote, 'and wife.' She slid the book back to the clerk, who now looked confused.

Then, in their rented room, he commanded, "Undress me." Then he did the same to her. Neither of them had any doubts about what was going to happen next!

He lay down on his back, expecting her to nestle next to him. Instead, she straddled over him. Ever so slowly she inserted him to her birth canal; slowly, slowly, while he enjoyed every moment of contact down to the last millimeter. Then, to Carter's surprise, his wife contracted her muscles around him, squeezed until she felt an answering pulse, then let go— *again!* Finally he had arched up to her, thrust deep within her, pulling her closer with his arms around her. There were no words for that kind of intense pleasure, only sounds. Then they nestled together.

Apparently there is something to be said for monogamy.

The door slammed. It was Carter, bearing his brief, full of other people's lives. One look at his wife led him to ask, "What's wrong?"

"Memories, memories. You have them too, don't you?"

"Of course. But listen. One of my colleagues has polo ponies and he is always complaining the cost to have them exercised during the week. I said you might be interested—was I wrong?"

"No!"

As for Carter, he comprehended he had used the wrong approach; a direct challenge over checkbooks had lit the fuse. Ever after, he used his judicial skill by asking himself, 'Can you rephrase that?"

C H A P T E R 6

Upon arriving home that afternoon, Carter went to his office to retrieve cash from the safe to pay for the hotel. He did not want to leave any traces; he had left his license with the manager as pledge he would return with pounds, although the manager told him he did not need to.

The fax machine had been busy while they were otherwise employed. The Sidi had sent through the relevant paperwork for MI6. He also added a small note asking Carter to call him through their secure line at Scotland Yard.

The familiar voice came through. "I've faxed the documentation to you, Carter, as this way I shall be sure MI6 receives it.

"As you iterated to me, MacGregor's supposition about two inebriated young rogue agents proved correct, so we were able to swiftly find our courier who had been handcuffed to a stanchion in a barn. I am sure the young men will be alarmed to find him gone.

"To return to the courier system, should MacGregor wish to, I shall suggest using the two erstwhile employees who would otherwise be discharged to act as couriers between MI6 and Jordan."

"I'm sure Ewen will entertain your suggestion; I don't know what he will conclude." *I'll find out.*

On Monday morning, Carter wrote a note. 'Could you stop at my chambers? I have something of yours.'

As he suspected, Ewen came straightaway—MsT. showed him into chambers, where a man was already seated on the sofa. Ewen had never met him, but intuited who it was as he encountered his worst nightmare: Sidi el Hassem, reading his pink *Financial Times*.

Dropping his copy of the newspaper, the Sidi asked in even, civil tones, "Mr. MacGregor, I presume?"

Ewen stuttered, "Why—yes! What are you doing here?"

"I moved my travel plans forward so as to see the person at the other end of our courier system." As he looked at Ewen his eyes narrowed slightly. Otherwise he remained congenial.

"Tea, Mr. MacGregor?"

"Please."

MsT., as Carter expressed it, made a mean cuppa. Using a pot, sugar, milk mug and cups from the china cabinet, she went about it in the classic way: first, pouring boiling water into the pot, swishing it around, then emptying it out, next, adding four scoops plus one for the pot to steep, kept warm under a tea cozy.

"Please!"

A rattle of tea cups marked Carter's entrance to the scene as MsT. took pot and accoutrements from the tray and placed three of them on two tables, and the last one on her desk. Then she poured. Ewen looked increasingly uncomfortable. Carter nodded to MsT. who handed MacGregor the faxed documents.

"I entered your premises, Carter, by the most secret way I could—"

"It will not escape the notice of the L.C.D," remarked the Sidi, who knew the initials stood for 'Lord Chancellor's Division.'

"Damn, Carter you've pinched me!"

"I am merely returning the favor—you lot caused me to create a postponement, which was totally unnecessary. It has backed up my schedule."

"Should that woman be present?"

Carter never doubted MsT.'s loyalty: during those 3 years, she would arrive early, waiting for him: her greeting "Good morning, judge!" sounded more like a sigh of relief than a greeting. She was mistress of the finishing touch; if one of the wraps around Carter's neck turned askew as he vested, her fingers would straighten and tuck at the recalcitrant piece of red or black or white fabric, or tie the black ribbons behind his neck.

This morning, he had on one of the suits and ties the Sidi had provided. It startled her so much she exclaimed, "Sir Carter!" She had been excited to finally meet that mysterious personage, the Sidi. He did not disappoint. He presented her with a box of homemade Bedouin sweets.

Carter had replied, "She stays, Ewen." He yanked off his wig, and shrugged out of his red robe and hung it up while she was busy placing the wig in its box. He was aware that Ewen was watching, for normally, a clerk would help a judge out of his paraphernalia.

"Ewen," he said, and shook hands. He sat down in an armchair.

He never knew that when the female clerks ate together, they would tease MsT. "You work for the youngest and sexiest judge in the building."

"And that's not saying much!" the senior clerk would always say, to the accompaniment of salvo of laughter. This cavalier treatment of her boss always was distasteful to MsT., and she suspected they knew it. However, the group did one thing which MsT. joined: it was called Loose Hands in the Hallway. And it contained ratings for the various Court personnel, so the women knew who to try to avoid. Carter was not one of them. From his own mother he had heard the occasional lament about this condescending practice.

They had elided MsT. to Misty. She was reserved but respected, congenial but not familiar; the three years' hiatus of safehousing had left her different from the other women; her tongue was never loose or gossipy. She never spoke about a current trial: loose lips sink ships. Frank Sinatra put it right: *won't dish the dirt with the rest of the girls*, and there was so much dirt to dish. As a group, she knew they took her silence as some kind of moral superiority, when it only simple security.

But now, she sat down at her desk, which she judged to be as out of the way as possible, as her boss stated, "I shan't rely on M.I.6 to police itself."

They both would not forget the days after his return, when she had said hesitantly, "Judge…"

"Righto, MsT."

"Are you saying a prayer before you take to the bench?"

"I am indeed, MsT.—a short one. I am more and more aware that our proceedings will change lives."

"I…there is something I should tell you so you cannot be surprised…"

"I am listening, MsT.—What is it?"

She drew back almost as she were afraid he might hit her. "Judge…I am not a heterosexual. What I am is forbidden in the Bible."

"I cannot pretend you take me totally by surprise."

"Why is that?"

"Never an evidence of a boyfriend."

"Will I go to Hell?

"Is that what you believe?"

"Sometimes I feel quite afraid."

"You must have a touch of prevenient grace to even ask that question, MsT."

"I'm not sure I follow you."

"It is Paschal's wager viz. whether you believe in the existence of God or not. You have already solved that part. I must confess it was never on my agenda to even ask that question. However, when we were flying to Texas, the powers that be decided to install another tank of petrol and use a special pilot to see if we could refuel a fighter jet. As the fighter jet came closer, I became convinced we were going to crash, and that I was seeing my death coming at me. It was the very first time I had opportunity to think of what might happen after I died, MsT., and I broke out in a cold sweat.

"But as it happened, this fear of Hell—for I'd led a sinful life—opened me to receive the grace which awaited me. You, on the other hand, are asking a question I experienced in a very short time. My besetting sin, fornication, is mentioned a good deal in the Bible, while I believe the first time the word homosexuality was mentioned was in 1946. Before that it was lumped under perversion, MsT."

"How would something like that happen to me?"

"The current Pope has said the most mercy will be shown to those living with a moral misery. I pray for mercy."

"Why?"

"My back pages are not illustrious, MsT. I was a bloody bastard as a barrister."

"So I've heard, Sir Carter."

"I cannot quote you chapter and verse. I was very struck by the words or Teresa of Avila, to wit, the feeling that God is journeying with us."

"And that means…?"

"We humans are not stationary. The old theory that all is unmovable has been disproved more than once—take the notion the earth was flat, or that the sun moved around the earth. God allows us to discover things about His creation. We now know that people are sometimes born with a mix of chromosomes. One thing I do like: 'when we practice prayer, not to be frightened by our own thoughts.' When you have doubts, remember that."

"So you'd say prayer is the…the *je ne sais quoi?*"

"A toss-up between prayer and love."

"Love, judge?"

"Your loyalty during very trying times bespeaks a loving heart, MsT. "

And MsT. thought she would not hear that kind of compliment anytime soon again.

"—would you ever have picked me as a likely stepfather for a little girl?"

"Well—"

"No, you wouldn't!" Carter laughed.

There was another day Ms.T highly anticipated. Valerie and Mercy came on the scene.

The day he had first come in with Mercy, who stood up on a chair and said "Hi," MsT. watched cautiously. It was only when

Valerie and Mercy entered chambers that she was better able to assess what she had been wondering—what kind of woman would marry her boss, and vice versa? MsT. involuntarily gawked at Valerie, who was wearing silver metallic boots with brown tracings, white jeans, and an ornate Texas shirt.

"Did you go to the soup kitchen with Mummy?" he asked.

"They love it when Mummy wears her Texas stuff." Mercy jumped onto the sofa and tucked her legs under her like a perching bird. Would the mother reprove her? She wondered.

Valerie said, "Take your shoes off, Mercy. Other people are going to sit there."

"How was the soup kitchen?"

"Oh, rather jolly. It's one of the days I tell our guests they can order whatever they want. They won't get it, but they can order it. There are some sophisticated palettes!"

"I put flowers on the table!" said Mercy.

Carter plucked her off the sofa. She knew what she was supposed to do; she walked over to MsT. and extended her hand. She and MsT. shook hands.

"Gee, you've got a lot of stuff on your desk!"

"Most of it will go to the Court of Appeals, tomorrow," said MsT. congenially. A green trolley became visible parked in a corner of the room, bearing a stack of boxes.

"We are asking for a new trial because new evidence has come to light—we have a witness willing to testify under the public interest immunity," Carter explained.

"Can I look?" Carter slid his chair back and set Mercy on his knees, so she was close enough to read some paperwork. The language was so dense and legal that the look was a short one. "Can my Poppy read this?" Startled by this innocent question, MsT. laughed.

The phone rang. MsT. answered, "Mr. Justice Braxton's chambers." She listened, then said to Carter, "It's Dame Barbara for you."

"Give her the top sheet," Carter said, as he picked up the receiver, putting a finger to his lips to shush Mercy. From his replies, they gathered he was ascertaining something.

"Yes, of course, it will be ready tomorrow and we shall send a copy by courier." He rang off and explained it was the Director of Crown Prosecutor Service, ringing to see if the appeal was ready.

"Appeals are rather rare. This is the first one we've ever had," he explained. "They are watching."

We've. Yes, Carter had spoken of MsT. in appreciative terms, but it had been a pass-by for me until today. Wonder why. Didn't want to? She could feel suppressed excitement in both of them. MsT. shared things with Carter she did not. *That's why I overlook her.* She knows when Carter is concentrating, he is so focused he does not hear what someone might be asking him, and she waits until his mind has relaxed. He really appreciates that.

There were parts of the legal calendar she enjoyed—the terms between when the Court sat. When the Court did sit, Carter was fully occupied, even putting in several overnights.

While Mercy carefully carried it across the room, he put on his reading glasses. He picked her up and settled her on his knees again, next to the desk surface.

"Poppy—is that Latin?"

"Yes, it is my little polyglot."

"What does this say?"

"*Rebus sic stanibus*, a plea that when certain circumstances change, it nullifies what has gone before."

"Oh! That's me!" She pointed to her photograph on his desk. "And Mummy's on the wall! And—is that Nate? Why is he wearing that funny hat?"

"He was my professor at Oxford, Mercy; he is wearing his academic robes."

"Can I have it?"

"No. I'll ask him for another." It was so old no one really recognized him, which was just the way he liked it.

CHAPTER 7

"Why do we professional chaps acquire such beastly writing?" grumbled Carter. "This looks to be written by a squirrel!"

"We start on the A1." Valerie was an ace at reading maps. After twenty miles with two turns, they arrived at the stable.

"Oh, how keen!" said Valerie. "This place is poshy!"

Carter had as a colleague Tony, a man with two polo ponies, who needed weekly exercise at an almost prohibitive cost.

The stable was built out of lovely wood (Valerie had to inspect it, of course), while the inside was spotless, a white cement floor down the middle. Looking down to the other end, there were rows of box stalls, each with a head peering out to see what was happening over the bronze label that bore his or her name.

"Oh, look!" said Valerie. "This is really interesting."

The wood took a lower dip about two feet from its elevation at the door, and the space created between stalls was filled in with slim iron bars which horses could see through. "What a good idea! They are social animals, you know. We should wait for your friend to show up, don't you think? It doesn't look like the kind of place where strangers can just walk in to look around."

"Yes, Tony's always a trifle late."

"Even for trials?"

Carter shrugged. "Give or take five or ten minutes." There was a screech of tyres turning in the driveway, then gravel thrown around by a fancy sports car, especially when the driver jammed on the brakes.

"Sorry, Carter, old chap! Pray introduce me!" Tony raced over to them. He was slim, perhaps five feet ten, with blond hair just beginning to thin on top, and dressed in breeches and a tweed coat, under which he wore a polo shirt.

"Tony Barton, my wife, Lady Valerie Falconer."

Tony looked confused.

"That is her *nom du boeuf,*" said Carter, with a smile.

"Oh, righto! Must be jolly fun to watch them turn out!"

"You've never seen her studio."

"You see, I mix all my own paint." Tony did not know what she meant, so he changed the subject.

"Shall we meet my ponies?"

Valerie had bought a brand-new polo shirt, and was wearing her white jodhpurs and well broken in old boots.

"Here they are," Tony said, although it was evident they recognized his voice, so stood waiting expectantly. They nuzzled on his top pocket, which produced two carrots, one for each.

"Are you at all familiar with polo, Lady Valerie?"

"Oh, yes, we've played it in Texas for a long time. Five persons to a team and slightly different rules. But Pop recalls his father loading up his ponies, driving to the match, playing the match, then immediately driving back home."

"Have you played?"

"When they couldn't find another substitute."

"What breed of horse do you use?"

"Oh, Morgans are the best at short sprints."

"We use thoroughbreds."

"Oh, their poor little thin legs would not hold up on our terrain."

Naturally, the grooming and saddling in such a place was done by stable boys, so Valerie watched the tack being put on. The saddle was similar to an old jumping seat, which had no leather curved forward from the pommel skirts as on a forward seat saddle. It was a stance reproduced in thousands of oil portraits in which the rider looked more as if he were seated on a sofa rather than a horse. Two reins, which Tony called, "snaffle and gig,"=a curb bit, she translated.

The lateral bridle strap which ran from ear to mouth divided into two pieces toward the bottom, one piece going to the snaffle bit, one to the gig bit; with a two-rein arrangement such as this one, the rider could pull on one rein harder than the other.

The first martingale strap around the horse's lower neck was attached to a horizontal strap which ran up to the bits and was held in place by two nosebands, while the lower martingale hooked onto a second girth which wrapped all the way around the horse, passing over the saddle. Tony saw Valerie eying this get-up.

"Yes, you must have good control!" he noted.

"All you need is a crupper," she replied. "I used to practice passing shots with my brother, Buddy. We learned to angle the mallet so as to make passing shots which could not cross the line of drive."

"Right. You see, Carter. Opposition may not pass over the line of drive—that is, a hypothetical extension of the direction in which the ball is traveling, Carter, except on rare occasions when the distance is great enough not to pose a danger to either rider."

"Must be bloody hell to be a referee."

The groom led one horse, a bay, fully groomed and saddled. "Oh, isn't he a lovely fellow!" *Look at all the tack on that horse. It must have cost a fortune.*

"I don't need all that equipment just to exercise the horse, do I?"

"Of course not. Thought I'd just show you the whole nine yards. My other pony is a mare. She is feisty. His name is Charlie. Do you want to take him for a turn inside the fencing?"

"Sure." Valerie headed over to the mounting block.

"Let's see. I think the stirrups ought to come up about two notches."

"That sounds right." Valerie moved her leg back so Tony could get under the saddle flap. *I'm glad they know what they are doing or I might have punched him in the nose for groping my wife.* Tony tugged on the thick stirrup strap until he reached access to changing the stirrup notches two holes.

"Righto. Now stand up in them. Yes, it looks right." He handed her the mallet, (which he called a polo stick) which had a striking face slightly slanted, shorter toward the horse, longer toward where it would brush the ground.

"What's this?" Valerie held up a loop.

"It goes around your thumb. It's called a slip. Luckily you are right -handed. OK. Let's go on the field. I'll fit you with spurs and a whip."

"Honey, would you bring me my hard hat?" While he picked it up, she moved her barrette from the top of her head to the back of her neck, with her hair hanging down her back, so as to fit the helmet onto her head. Last, she donned a pair of wrap-around plastic glasses to keep dust out of her contact lenses. She touched her whip to her hat, then off she went.

Tony and Carter stood at the outside of the rail, the inevitable one foot up on the bottom plank.

"I say, Carter, I didn't know you were interested in horses."

"I'm not. All I know about them is you feed one end and muck out at the other."

"You know, I've filed for a divorce."

"So I heard."

"The damn thing is, it is so repetitious it became boring. What about you? I've heard on the Q.T. your wife has some kind of— discernment? Is that the right word?"

"Of course. After all, she married me!"

"She could become a good substitute player."

"Don't even think about it."

"May I ask you a personal question?"

"You can try."

"I heard tell in your younger days you were quite a ladies' man. What do you feel like now?"

"I realized at one point I always had to have at least two scotches before I shagged a new woman."

"Meaning—?" said Tony thoughtfully.

"I needed to get below a level which normally the individual can control. How many times have we heard 'I did it under the influence?'"

"Many, many times."

Just then, Valerie turned, and came back toward them at a full gallop. "Oh lord, I hope she has Charlie under control!" exclaimed Tony. She waited until the last moment to rein him in. She was laughing.

"Well, he certainly knows where the barn is!" she said.

"Want to try the mare?"

"Righto." Off she went again on a chestnut-colored mare.

"Val gave me a place in the universe, Tony. I had no family save for some elderly friends. Now I have abundant family, in fact, soon I will become a grandfather."

"So that changes the libido?"

"For the better," said Carter, with a laugh.

CHAPTER 8

Carter had promised to meet the Archbishop of Westminster, who had asked if they could meet so as to better understand what had happened in order to field questions from parishioners and the public.

Carter treated himself to a ride on the top of a bus, where he could watch a hypothetical crash into the trees approaching as it turned a corner. Happily he climbed down, crossing a pleasant piazza of wide pieces slate filled with children playing, roller skating, skateboarding, adults reading the paper, or taking a smoke while eating lunch, until he mounted the steps and looked around him in the comparative darkness. He moved slowly from the entrance, passed by the carved wooden choir stalls, up toward the altar in the front. He was confused, because, although the bottom of the cathedral, running about half-way up, it was nicely decorated, the arch of the roof seemed a solid dirty color, as if it had never been finished. He heard a rustle of a long skirt behind him; turning, he met a more practical head dress than the starched and winged ones that proclaim Rome wasn't built in a day.

"Sir Carter?"

"Yes, sister?"

"Please follow me."

"Gladly, sister."

There was a bookstore attached to the cathedral, which opened into a warren of offices. Walking back to the entrance to access the bookstore, she showed him an exit at the back, announcing briefly,

"Sir Carter, Your Grace."

"Thank you, sister," said the man behind the desk as he stood up. Being a captive of regalia himself, Carter let his eye wander over the bishop's accoutrement; a long black gown, with red buttons down the front, accented by red piping at the edge; a shoulder caplet also edged with red piping, a violet waistband and skullcap, a cross whose chain crossed his chest, a Roman collar. He rose to greet his visitor with a handshake, offered him a chair before resuming his seat behind his desk.

"What color purple is that?" asked Carter.

"Mauve, violet, magenta…I'm not sure. I've always been curious about the wigs you chaps wear. Are they hot?"

"Rarely, but they are made of horsehair, so from time to time, a stalk wiggles through—then I fold my pocket handkerchief and put it on my head under where the damn thing is poking me."

"I thank you for coming. Let me present my opinion, it may save us some time. Being a Roman, I am able to take in the evidence of a healing if I see one. The man was definitely crippled; now he can walk; you are a witness to it. What else could produce such an effect? Did you ever read Sherlock Holmes as a boy?"

"Didn't everyone? Whatever you are left with, no matter how incredible, is the truth?"

"Righto. I noticed your finesse in using the term 'alleged' miracle. Remarkably fortuitous. We seem to be nearly on the same page. Would you mind if I have got these events straight? I gather that when you and your wife were in a suburb of Cairo, visiting a Muslim friend, what has been termed a miracle occurred.

"I wanted to meet you because I will have people on my doorsteps for months asking about it—atheists who think it is bunkum, Protestants who believe in dispensationalism, scientists asking for clear evidence, the faithful, who are either happy or doubtful, those who believe this was a *deus ex machina* from the Heavens because doubt is eating into faith on earth too deeply, not to mention parish crazies.

"One main battle line, as you probably realize, is going to be how this apparition is titled. To the Orthodox and the Catholics, the Blessed Virgin Mary. Not so to the Muslims, Jews, or Protestants. However, I am happy say the Coptic Orthodox church will have to deal with it—it's in their jurisdiction. Were you surprised?"

"Actually, my wife lives with the principle of what C.S. Lewis calls the 'rules beyond the rules,' so virtually by now nothing surprises me anymore."

"May I ask why you were in Zeitoun in the first place?"

"I am not sure how much I wish to say about that, as it is not my story, but the Sidi's. But, in general, the Sidi has made pilgrimages to the spot at St. Mary's Coptic Church in Zeitoun where the apparition of a woman appeared over a three-year period, in the late 1960's and early 70's, who has been titled Our Lady of Zeitoun. He said she drew him back time and again as if she were a magnet. He is very devoted to her, as he saw Jews, Orthodox, Muslims, and Christians come in devotion and peace with each other to a spot where many healings occurred."

Carter was reaching for his inside jacket pocket when his hand touched the piece of paper from his front lawn. He pulled it out and smoothed it.

"Good Lord! I forgot this!" he laid it on the Archbishop's desk top. "Do you know what this is?"

"Certainly. It is a witchcraft symbol."

"How could I have forgotten it for two days?"

"As John of the Cross notes, 'the devil hides most easily in the human memory. Did he call upon the Lady for healing?"

"No, he had accepted his situation. Apparently she thought otherwise."

"Before we go any further, is it possible to talk by phone with your friend?"

Carter looked at his watch. "I think we can just. But I will have to contact Scotland Yard for a connection. Would you mind?" Carter dialled the number. "I don't know how long—"

But the telephone rang back immediately, as if a plan were falling into place.

"Sidi!"

"My dear friend!"

"I am with the Archbishop of Westminster. He has asked if he might speak to you about the apparition."

There was silence. The Archbishop waited patiently, knowing it was a most sensitive question to ask, and the Sidi must await a word of conclusion.

Finally, the Sidi said, "On his honor, as long as it goes no further."

"It will be under the seal of the confessional, Sidi, which means it cannot be disclosed even under pain of death."

"I see. Most interesting. You know, I am sure, that the Koran speaks with approbation about your Virgin Mary."

"Yes."

"This is not her for me, although it might well be she that Christianity worships; I do not speculate upon such mysteries. For me, she is Lady Wisdom, the one the Lord set up before the beginnings of the earth. She who possesses wisdom and strength. She who blesses the children of Abraham."

The Archbishop gave a small whistle.

"It is she who desires the children of Abraham to realize their common origin."

"This conversation is, I remind you, under the seal of the confessional! But I certainly look forward to meeting you. Your friend Justice Braxton has just brought in a witchcraft sign dropped on his lawn.

"As you may or may not know," said the Archbishop, "in our European tradition, each monastery has an exorcist. In mine I have that role. I am an abbot on interim assignment until the Vatican picks a replacement. In this way, I have a chance to observe the culture outside our monastery. For instance, I've heard a worrisome rumor that the Anglican church wished to strike 'I renounce the devil and all his works,' from their baptismal creed. Do not worry about your friend." They exchanged formal farewell greetings.

Jules Latham rang off, asking Carter, "Would you mind if I offered you general absolution? You have been unchurched for many years. General absolution is in general for your sins, not a personal one. It lifts the feeling of the lens of sin, so you can see the world in what I can only call a more Christocentric light. You know that persons who work in the area where demons dwell need a clean conscience."

"I don't think Valerie has got to telling me that yet. She did say I should leave the room if I started to feel any fear or doubt."

"It is a sensitive subject."

As he was about to leave, the Archbishop said, "I hear the Archbishop of Canterbury has respectfully requested the Patriarch of the Coptic Orthodox Church to share copies of the x rays with him."

"Why ever?"

"About what you'd expect—British Anglicans involved."

As they shook hands at the door, the Archbishop said, "We should deal with this immediately, Sir Carter. May I come round to your home in full regalia tonight?"

"It would be an honor."

"Shall we say tonight at six o'clock?"

C H A P T E R   9

Sure enough, at precisely 6 p.m. a car drew up; the Archbishop stepped out, not yet in full regalia, with an assistant carrying his bishop's mitre, staff, and a censor, meanwhile, the bishop himself was carrying a bottle of holy water and a book whose title was in Latin.

As he stepped upon the pavement, the whole family—Jane included—came out to greet him. A crowd began to gather as the Archbishop used the censor to sprinkle the house with water, then incensed it. Last, he sprinkled a surprised Carter, Valerie and Mercy liberally with water.

Is it my imagination or did he douse us with particular zest?

"Can you do that for my house?" a woman demanded.

"Come and talk to me about it first."

Then he turned to the continually assembling group. "Do I understand there is a malevolent presence on this street?"

The people nodded their heads or mumbled, "Yes." He held up Carter's latest missive. "Does this look familiar?" Again, quiet methods of assent.

"I am going to walk down this street reading traditional prayers and I am going to clean the atmosphere. I would appreciate it if any of you are brave enough to accompany me." Instantly Carter, Valerie, and Mercy fell in line, as Carter advised Jane not to participate.

"Go inside, so your mother will not see you."

Then the Archbishop's assistant robed him in a garment full of lace and good tailoring, placed a stole around his neck with a cross on each of the four sides, a pectoral cross, the zuchello on his head, and handed him his staff.

"*Crois que nous serions prêt.*" So his companion was a monk. His assistant lighted the incense; at close range, Carter sneezed, his eyes stung, and he was disinclined to breathe.

I hope there was not enough frankincense to gas the baby Jesus.

Mercy began to cough! But the assistant moved away, spreading incense to the four winds by swinging it in all directions with the chains to which it was attached.

Turning to face the people who had assembled, the Archbishop spoke. "The principle effect these little symbols have created is to spread fear up and down the street. It was palpable to me as I turned the corner. Fear prevents one from being able to achieve his or her goals. Also, in this case, it was a weapon which intimidated anyone from complaining about conditions in this woman's home and with her child.

"As we walk down the street, I will be reading from the Roman ritual, also I will asperse front lawns unless anyone asks me not to. Let those who can sing do so."

The Archbishop began his walk down the street. His assistant held the book and illuminated it from a pocket torch. After he read, he would sprinkle. Valerie started the Battle Hymn of the Republic, known to both British and Americans. The Archbishop paused at every house he came to, sprinkled the lawn and said a prayer.

"Walk with me, Carter, there will be no reporters."

How does he know that?

Bit by bit, the rest of the people on the street lost their fear of joining the procession. Some began to sing.

As they neared Mrs. Collins's house, she came out, slamming the front door, half dressed, half *en negligee,* a bit the worse for her evening's libations. Her voice became shrill as she hurled imprecations at them. Some of the people stopped, and appeared to be drifting away. The Archbishop stepped close to her, and sprinkled her with holy water, and she began to scream.

"They don't like holy water," he told Carter.

I'll remember that.

CHAPTER 10

On Monday morning, John Hawkins of the Metropolitan Police called him.

"Carter, do you know the Collins woman on your street has filed assault charges against you?"

When he told Valerie, she said, "So that's what it is!"

"What do you mean?"

"It's hard to explain, but at times I see a faint shadow before me, indicating that something which smacks of evil is about to occur—and at times, it starts to move closer,—but not yet this time."

"Would you like us to ring to see if she has second thoughts?" John Hawkins asked.

"Oh, no, no! Favor me and get her to write a complaint statement by hand. You have copies of the notes from our lawn."

"I don't think, frankly, they are written by the same person."

"Righto. I'll send both to handwriting section, then get a match of both Mrs. Collins's and our anonymous note-writer."

"Thank you, John."

"We do receive reports here of places where witchcraft ceremonies have taken place. Generally only animal sacrifice. But once a young lady ran after me, terrified and trembling, asking if I could help her, as she had been designated a bride of satan."

"What did you do?"

"I safehoused her."

John Hawkins had known Carter for some years. When Carter was a young barrister, he awkwardly stumbled into the local police station and asked if someone could take him through the police processes. John was the youngest recruit on duty, so naturally they palmed him off to deal with this surprising nuisance. John was uneasy, expecting to be condescended to, thus he was hoping it would be a fast once over. Carter took in the chevrons on his sleeve and watched, with a great sense of ritual, as he donned the iconic police helmet.

Little could John know Carter was more at home at the station than in the court, finding himself on more familiar ground than John had expected—after all, Carter was from a rough neighborhood where the police were scarcely unknown entities.

As for Carter, he found John far more intelligent and efficient than he had anticipated. John discovered this was not a photo op tour. His guest examined everything, and was allowed to watch an interrogation through the one-way glass. He asked questions John did not know the answers to as yet.

John smiled. *All right, bright boy, I'll give you the complete tour.* "How would you react to spending the day shift me on Saturday? Foot patrol, you know."

"I'll bring my running shoes."

How different to go street by street on foot. First was a halloo from an elderly lady. "You hoo! Constable Hawkins! Can you help me—I can't find my hand bag." John went right to work, giving Carter time to absorb the flat.

It was very tidy, with not too much chintz. A rack on the wall contained ceremonial dishes issued on special occasions; the one he first noted was from the coronation of Elizabeth II. A cozy sofa, with an orange and white cat at one end, asleep; it lay next to a ball of yarn with knitting needles thrust into it. Above the couch was a cross stitch sampler which read 'a stitch in time saves nine.' He had to ask.

"Ma'am, is your cat named Stitch?"

"How very clever, young man."

Meanwhile, John had found her pocket book wedged between a cushion and the back of the sofa. She clutched it to her bosom and thanked him profusely.

"Would you like some tea?"

"Emily, love, alas, but I'm on duty."

They said their farewells and resumed their walk on the pavement.

"She is a full-on-dear," John remarked, as they descended the stairs.

Carter was pondering how this allocation of resources for Emily would look in a duty book.

"She can't find her own handbag?"

"Look at the woman, Carter. She is frail. Not fit to be moving furniture. I dread the day she either passes or goes to a nursing home—she's a safe harbor on rotten days. And yes—we are here to help, and keep an eye on our aging citizens."

You'd feel differently if it were your Mum.

Carter never forgot that answer.

"Now when we turn the corner, there is a pub where a number of chaps start the day early. They are a dodgy lot."

Sure enough, the pub was already filled to capacity so people were standing on the sidewalk with their mugs. Carter noticed John had his truncheon out and was tapping it lightly on his open left hand.

"Hey there!" he was welcomed with a bit too much false heartiness.

"Come now, boys, you know you are not to gather into a cluster, but leave a pathway so people can use the pavement."

One customer has obviously been there from the moment the pub had opened, and was already in a foul mood.

"I ought to give you a bunch of fives, I'm so tired of you pushing us around." Carter saw his hand tighten into a fist, the arm pulled back to throw a punch; forgetting his instructions to stay put, he started to run to John's aid. He need not have worried.

"Are you now?" John pulled back his truncheon and plunged it into the man's abdomen, completely knocking the wind out of him, at which point he fell to the pavement. John stepped inside and informed the bartender that the taxi company would send a bill for the fare to him as they wrestled their inebriate into a taxi.

John had noticed how Carter always hesitated for just an instant before he spoke, as if he were collecting himself. He decided to ask a question. "Which university did you graduate from?

"Oxford."

John paused for a moment, then, said, jokingly, "It's an honor, sir!"

"I'm not a sir."

"But you will be."

"Until then, call me Carter."

And John was present the day Carter was knighted—first in line to call him, 'Sir!'

John wrestled with his conscience, for Carter was, indeed, hard to figure. He could find out from his birth certificate: but was it proper to spy upon one's associates? Finally he succumbed, however, to investigating Carter's background and pulled up his birth certificate.

Good Lord! That good man thought. Now he realized he could not keep it secret from his new friend. Otherwise, it would stand like a wall between them. Cannily—or so he thought—he drove by the hospital where his new friend had been born, and pointed it out, hoping Carter would reply in kind.

When Carter didn't, John said, "I must confess I looked in General Records to see where you were born."

"Why didn't you say? If you hadn't, you wouldn't be half the detective I think you are!"

C H A P T E R   1 1

With a trial date set, social workers made a survey of the Collins' house. The shades were always drawn, which gave the house a somber lighting, so they had no idea what to expect.

"Good Lord," said one worker to the other, "They could film the Addams family here!"

There were unwashed dishes piled in the sink, clean clothes dumped in a lump on the dining room table; dust and a few cobwebs. Upstairs, they gingerly lifted the cover on Jane's bed, which revealed hideously unwashed sheets. The bathroom was strewn with drying stockings; the bathtub was more or less untouched by cleaning. Last, there was Jane, in an unwashed dress, untowardly thin, undoubtedly verbally, if not physically abused. They wrote a report to the effect she should be removed to foster care, if possible.

He explained what was going to happen plainly to Jane after dinner that night. She was distressed to being moved to someplace with which she was unfamiliar, let alone unknown people.

"Just hold up and be brave. It will only be for a little while, for your mother has charged me with assault. I want you out of her reach until that is settled. Can you tell me, Jane, who the man is who comes Thursday nights who either gives or takes something from your mother?"

"Oh, mother gives our money to him."

"Why?"

"I don't really know. It has something to do with taking over the earth. She writes it all down in a notebook she keeps in her top desk drawer. She says then we live in a golden palace."

Meanwhile, the assault trial proceeded in record time so as to get Carter back on the bench. Tony would be his lawyer; on the first day, Carter walked into High Court as neither barrister nor a judge, but as the defendant in the dock standing, answering with the calling of his name. Although judges do not have to take the oath, he did so anyway. When the judge entered, as he bowed his head, and sat at his place, it was to him as if he were seeing a mirror image.

Did Mrs. Collins see the defendant here present? He felt awkward to be pointed out again. Then came the questions and the action he was charged with. "Sir Carter, you are charged…How do you plead?" He stood up. A zany thought filtered through his mind. *What would happen if I pled guilty?*

He saw the stenographer beginning to take notes, and the court sketcher getting to work. All the formalities of court he'd grown inured to now registered like thunder claps: the jury, called by name, then administered the oath, 'I swear to faithfully discharge…'Tony entering a motion to permit him to sit at the defence table instead of the dock, which was granted. The announcement, "I now call the Crown to proceed with the case."The judge was an old hand, taciturn, "not a showboat," as Valerie phrased it.

Valerie had been already seated in the spectators' gallery above the court floor. Carter had told her Tony's wife might come; Valerie thought she might be curious to see the woman who exercised her husband's ponies. Also in the spectator's gallery were an odd assortment of people obviously here to support the prosecuting of the case; they were an odd enough lot that Valerie began to feel the shadow was moving closer.

She had never been to court to observe a case before. Soon enough, an unknown voice asked, "Are you Braxton's wife?"

Cordially, Valerie replied, "Yes, Valerie Falconer."

"Falconer?"

"Yes, it is my late husband's name under which I began what Carter calls my *nom du boeuf,* as I paint the stickers to put on our Herrington beef. Would you like to slide in?" Without a reply, Tony's wife merely sat down.

Now Valerie could see her who had heretofore been only a voice behind her. Yes, one of those petite Englishwomen who could carry a minimum of flesh on their slender bones, dressed at the height of fashion, in a designer suit which cut off just above the breast.

Elegantly dressed brown hair; only the modicum of make up as was daytime proper. *Ah, she just isn't able to read me because she can't put me in a category. Like the frustrations of the British merchant bankers who did not understand why Texas bankers did not wear pink socks.*

The prosecutor stated their charge and immediately, to everyone's surprise, put Mrs. Collins on the witness stand.

Carter whispered to Tony, "The barrister is better than she could afford. Who is paying, I wonder?"

Mrs. Collins told her tale in words that would have made a rock cry—she, a single mother, unexpectedly set upon by a male neighbor. One of the jurors wiped her eyes.

Then a surprise—the neighbor across the street agreed.

Now Tony stood to plead for the defence. "Was she a good mother who kept a clean house?" The neighbor replied, "Yes."

'Someone's gotten to him,' Carter scribbled in a note while Tony inclined his bewigged head, 'yes indeed.'

"Have you been induced to give evidence?" Tony asked. "Are you cognizant of the concept of perjury?"

"Permission to consult, milord." The prosecution barrister huddled with the witness and Mrs. Collins for a moment. Mrs. Collins found if she lied under the oath, she could be charged with perjury—as did her cooperative neighbor.

"Mr. George," the judge asked the prosecutor, "are you cross examining your own witness?"

"No, milord, simply explaining a concept of law."

The witness sat down and Tony called Mrs. Collins to the stand again. "Was it true that the defendant had simply come to invite her daughter to dinner?"

"Remember you are still under oath. The answer should be a simple yes or no," ruled the judge.

"Yes."

"Was the defendant standing on your pavement taller than you were, standing on the door stoop?"

The barrister huddled briefly with the neighbor. "No, milord, she was the taller."

The witness sat down and Tony called Mrs. Collins to the stand again. "Was it true that the defendant had simply come to invite her daughter to dinner?"

"Yes."

"And did you break a bottle on the door jamb and use the ragged edges as a weapon?"

"I certainly did!" she replied indignantly.

"You swung at the judge and cut his neck open?"

"Damn right I did."

"Please remember the injunction to simply answer 'yes,' or 'no,' and is it true you inflicted a diagonal cut across his neck?"

"Yes."

"Pardon, milord," said the prosecutor. "How is the jury expected to ascertain whether this cut at the neck occurred or not?"

Carter was beginning to feel a nervous discomfort, and against all his notions of the sanctity of a child, he was now glad Jane's name was on the list.

"I believe we have the means to demonstrate that," said Tony. Exhibit A. It was Carter's bloodstained shirt and the shards of glass and fabric.

"Now to further demonstrate the account of the event, if it please the court, I have asked for a ladder to be brought in."

"Oh, he's not going to!" his wife hissed. "I will never live this down."

"I believe he is," Valerie whispered.

"So granted," ruled the judge.

Tony unrolled an architectural diagram of the front porch area. "Now," he asked one of the clerks, "would you kindly climb the ladder to the red rung, which would have been the top of Mrs. Collin's head."

There was a hush in the court. Carter indicated Tony should go ahead. "Would my client be kind enough to show the jury the scar?" He would. He also glanced up toward his wife, and focused on her to help him through a rather humiliating moment. Tony helped Carter out of his jacket and necktie, then unbuttoned the first three upper buttons of his shirt.

"I am going to mark this scar with a red pencil so it is clearly visible to the jury. Now, the officer will be kind enough to hold one end of the string at the height of Mrs. Collin's head, and angle it to the bottom, where the judge was standing on the diagram?

"Can you stand there so we have the exact height?" Tony asked his client.

Oh, brilliant Tony! The angle was identical.

"You're having too much fun," Carter muttered. "Why did you pull this stunt?"

"Oh, I have photographs of your scar, but this was better," said Tony with a smile.

You owe me one, Tony!

"I'll never live this down," Tony's wife muttered again.

"Why not? I thought it was rather brilliant."

She sniffed. Certainly Sir Carter Braxton had married a peculiar wife.

"I will call our first witness, Dr. John Wilson."

Jack stood up and took the oath.

"Is it true that the defendant's wife asked him to have you come to your house to dress this wound?"

"Yes."

"Could you kindly tell us what it was?"

"A slash to the neck about seven inches long, administered with considerable force, which left glass fragments in the wound, which I proceeded to pick out. May I add it passed close to the ceratoid artery, in which case, without immediate assistance, the defendant would have bled to death. Glass shards from the blow are included under Exhibit A."

"Thank you, you may step down."

"Thank you, milord."

"Does the defence have more witnesses?"

"May I approach?" Tony asked once more, while the judge pulled his list of witnesses up on his computer.

"Milord, you'll notice a Jane Collins listed as a witness. This is Mrs. Collins' ten-year-old daughter. If it please the court, there is a video of her testimony in the judge's computer. The witness understands she is under oath, but we analysed this as the only way possible for her to be a witness against her own mother in open court. Milord, you will notice I am sitting beside her during this complete testimony."

"Chambers, gentlemen. The jury can relax, but stay nearby. The court stands adjourned until the return of the jury."

The usher showed the jury out. Tony and the prosecutor followed the judge. Chambers indicated the need to discuss this request in private. The judge also had it in his chambers' computer.

"Give me a legal reason why this video should be allowed as evidence."

"Milord, it can be substituted if the witness is either vulnerable or intimidated, or a child. All these apply, as well as does the fact the child suffers bouts of post-traumatic stress disorder as a result of her experiences."

I didn't realize that. Poor girl.

The prosecutor had no ready response. The video was conclusive and damaging.

So back in the courtroom once again, Tony made his closing statement, to wit, that this charge was a frame up which the evidence did not support. Tony pronounced the words, "I rest my case," the jury retired to consider a verdict.

They returned in half an hour. Judging from the crumbs still present on their persons, some had even had time to wolf down a scone or two. Tony made his closing.

"Has the jury reached a verdict?"

"Yes."

"Do you find the defendant guilty or not guilty?"

"We find the defendant not guilty."

"I will let that stand unless appeal is made, in which case I will introduce a prosecution for libel." Tony sat down.

Carter stood and heard his own sigh of relief, a sound he heard many times before as the verdict was announced.

"You are free to go," the judge said; after the court cleared, he stepped down to shake Carter's hand. "I am honored to have conducted a trial upon which a judge was the defendant," he said with a smile.

"I wonder why she brought such a weak case," Tony exploded.

"To embarrass me, old lad!" Carter replied.

Carte walked slowly to the door, afraid he had embarrassed Valerie, a notion quickly dispelled when she rushed over to kiss him. "Oh, how I wish Pop could have been here! He would have loved it. I wrote a note to the sketcher, asking to purchase the original. It will look swell on your chamber wall!"

"Braxton certainly has a peculiar wife," Tony's wife whispered to him.

"Oh, well, she's an American.

Now John and Carter were older. More experienced. John had been made a plainclothes Detective Sergeant, then climbed the ranks. Today, however, although he was used to the judge's smooth, now unhesitant speaking voice, yet he noticed something a bit different, something implacable.

"How well do you know her next door neighbor?"

"Not well. Just to halloo."

"Could we mount an infra-red camera on the side of his house?"

"I'll ring him tonight." His neighbor was more than agreeable. "It will be a dummy truck which says it installs telly satellites," Carter told him. "We'll procure a real one for your trouble."

"Splendid!"

"I'd guess we'd only get the courier," said Hawkins.

"Probably, you then could tail him?"

"Rental car."

"You still could see the number plates!"

"You've been watching too much telly. The rental agent has taken down all sort of information. He opens a book for us and gives you all the information you want—name, address, telephone number. Our courier probably paid in cash with a forged driving license. He probably gave the dealer a bribe to keep his mouth shut."

Thursday night the camera captured a male figure, car and number plate. To Carter's surprise, Hawkins was over the moon to receive it!

"If we are to pull off this stunt yet are unable to pick up information at one end, we certainly can at the other," John said.

"Meaning?"

"We have the infra-red camera next to Mrs. Collins, so, while that is helpful, it is unable to follow the car when it pulls away."

"But my NOMAD scanner can follow it, as long as I am in range of the car."

"You will be in the chase car?"

For several nights Carter went to bed fully clothed, and when the telephone rang, he sprinted out the back door around the corner to meet John in his car on the street that ran perpendicular to theirs.

"Follow 1988 red Ford, Number Plate, F134 KGN."

"What if he switches cars?" asked John.

"Then you get me close enough so I can read off the number plate."

John laughed.

Sure enough, when the suspect pulled into the rental agency, he switched out of the loaner vehicle to his own car. They followed him home.

John was pleased, but would have been more pleased if there were a reason to arrest him.

CHAPTER 13

Carter had thought all of it was over, but when the phone rang, Carter's whole world exploded. Would he come to the Lord Chancellor's office at ten o'clock tomorrow? A creeping dread began to spread through him, a sense of malevolence. The harder he tried to shake it off, the more intense it became.

At breakfast, he was tight lipped; Valerie asked him what was wrong.

"Oh, I've just been asked to see the Lord Chancellor, some little bit of business, that's all."

She knew full well what kind of unknown circumstances still hung over him, even after his long, distinguished career so, during morning devotions, when his mind was clearly elsewhere, she resisted asking him what was wrong, for that approach made him yet more insecure before he knew what it *was* that was wrong. She'd seen that a look on his face before, when he feared he had made a social gaffe, only quadruple. He did not ask her to tie his necktie, one of their romantic rituals.

The shadow was moving closer.

Once, the shadow had turned into night, and for 48 hours, all Valerie had seen in that 48 hours was night, while everyone else around her went merrily along in daylight during those days, while she saw it all through a nocturnal veil. At first, she had thought everything had turned to night; then she slowly noticed that outside, life was going about its daily business. She did not know what it meant, but it did not last the prophetic 3 days of darkness—the last night came a week later. She always prayed it would never happen again. She watched him walk out to his waiting car; the usual spring in his step was not there. His chauffeur let him off about a quarter of a mile from their destination so he could walk a bit, breathe, get his body moving, passing the little park with its incongruous statue of Abraham Lincoln on the left (*now there's a chap who had to steer his own course no matter how it ruffled people*) while to the right, a few more steps on, lay Westminster Abbey; he passed its side façade which led to the turn in the road which marked his destination.

"He'll be with you in a minute." He tried to focus on the office: behind the Chancellor's chair was a window, one red curtain pulled back to open on the scene he had just traversed. The portrait of the Queen swathed in the official ermine, the heavy crown of state on her head. *No wonder she gets headaches from wearing that thing.* At last, the Chancellor's portrait, in his full uniform, red, massed with gold.

Footsteps in the hallway. Carter stood up to shake hands. He realized the Chancellor probably still held resentments about having to push him up to judge.

"Coffee? Tea?" The inevitable formalities.

They each took a seat.

"We find ourselves on the horns of a dilemma."

You could certainly say that.

"We have had to lay on a few more bobbies at High Court, to push the lines across the street behind the barricades, for we get curious little crowds waiting to see if they can get a glimpse of you. Generally, they often hold divergent religious opinions, which they do not hesitate to express rather loudly, making the whole place a sort of debate society akin to Hyde Park. In short, they linger."

Carter knew very well what was being described. Small groups of people usually greeted him at his entrance to the Court of Justice, some for, some against. Some tried to touch his sleeve. Usually, the opened ranks for him, yet some mornings, he had to push his way through with a bobby.

He had finally arrived at his own idea of making an entrance. He said nothing, just raised his hat to the gathering, but stayed silent, knowing full well that even four words from him would be debated and misinterpreted twenty times by the evening news. One morning, a woman held out her baby to him. Alarmed, Carter simply touched his hat to her.

"But there have been demonstrations before when the police had to be called in," he pointed out. "They SIMPLY ordered people to stand behind the barricade."

"True. But then, the real question is how much this experience in Egypt might have affected your impartiality, and the public's opinion of your being biased."

Carter remarked, "There was quite a fracas during the oil bunkering trial, but I do not recall anyone complaining."

"Yes, yes, I am aware how much your service held for the Crown."

"Is it so threatening to have ONE judge out of the whole High Court people might consider to be 'religious?'"

"It is a moot point, I'm afraid. Many of the judges, whether rightly or wrongly, feel this may undermine the dignity of the court to have a morning crowd, not to mention going on trial for assault. And you can be sure more cases will come which deal with homosexuality, which your Christian faith condemns. Some members of High Court are asking you to consider if it might be wise for you to tender your resignation.

"We will hold a meeting this afternoon to try to discern how much sentiment here is for this point of view. Would you be good enough to come back again tomorrow morning, same time?"

"You have no legal reason to ask for my resignation."

"No—we are simply conveying the opinion of your peers as to the nuisance it's become."

"Ten o'clock then?" Picking up his trench coat, turning on his heel, leaving without the usual obsequious farewells, he addressed the deity: *God, up there in heaven with all your power and might, couldn't you aid me against the opinions of my peers?*

He decided to conduct his afternoon trial, which restored his fractured dignity slightly. MsT. evidenced notice that she perceived something was wrong, yet said nothing; nor did he speak. The afternoon jury came back with what he considered a reasonable charge, so at least he felt he had conducted a balanced trial.

Then he sat in his office with no lights on. MsT. had gone home. He sensed everything about his office: the rows of leather-bound books, the tea tray which was still breathing smells of Earl Gray; the wood of his desk with a pile of papers on it. *Goodbye to all that?* He asked, as he tried to steady himself to go home.

When he arrived home, he asked Valerie to come upstairs. Although Mercy was not home yet, he did not want her overhearing anything about this if she did arrive while they were talking.

"Val, what am I to do?"

"Beat the devil! I see a shadow before me coming closer: the dark powers are on the move. Damn it! I'll call Nate."

_C H A P T E R 1 4_

When ten a.m. came, a police car pulled up to the Chancellor's Department; first, Carter got out, then, reaching back into the car, he extended a strong elbow to an elderly man who was bent, fragile, stooped, yet wearing an old, but beautifully kept-up plush fedora which had been brushed carefully every day, a dark suit and black trainers (sneakers) for superior traction.

The elder man gripped his cane tightly to exit the vehicle, then two men then proceeded at a shuffling pace up the stairs, the older man with a cane on one side, Carter's arm to lean upon on the other. The latter's eyes misted over slightly as he saw the gold cuff links, a present from his sons, glittering on his shirt cuffs.

A small crowd had gathered, for Mildred had filed a column on the circumstances. Who was the elderly man? One member of the crowd exclaimed, "Why, that's Nathan Levi!"

"I thought he was dead!" A murmur swept through the crowd.

"Have you a wheelchair?" Carter asked at the top of the stairs. Yes, there was one; his unknown companion was content to ride as far as the Chancellor's office, yet at that point, he insisted on standing up, and walking down the aisle beside Carter.

They could see confusion on the faces of the men already seated in the room; finally, one of them whispered, "My God, it's Nathan Levi."

There was shuffling and whispering when confronted by this considerable surprise; his body was decomposing, but his mind was as clear as ever, and, as everyone realized, still the sharpest legal mind in the room. It was probable that some of the current judges had read his opinions, or even used text books he had written while at Oxford.

The Chancellor cleared his throat. He was reading from a piece of paper. "I will render our opinion, Sir Carter, then you will be allowed to reply. As you know, I control both judicial and ecclesiastical appointments, and while we do hope some appropriate accommodation can be made of your judicial skills, we do recommend you step down from the bench!"

"He's just described a partial theocracy!" Nate whispered to him, with a delight so obvious the judges stirred uneasily.

Now it was Carter's turn. "My Lords and learnèd fellow judges, it is well known that a judge can be asked to resign, but only for immoral, indecent, or criminal acts, such as adultery, which will place a permanent stain on their records."

He looked at the lineup in front of him, noting that several of them he knew from his bad old days had high color in their faces. "I am sure Miss Stevenson will be only too happy to follow up on them." *That's one thing I stayed clear of; married women—too many possible confrontations.*

"Since this is not the case, but merely a collection of opinions as to whether my fellow judges want me in High Court, I don't give a fig for their preferences—I do my job, to the point of being safehoused for three years. Find another judge who has done so. I suggest we at least consider a compromise; else I will sue the court for defamation of character."

"What do you have in mind, Sir Carter?"

"I will take it upon myself to step down for six months, and absent myself from the public. By then, I think this will have blown over."

Whispering and consulting among his judges. "A generous and a thoughtful answer—however—it does not match our conclusion. You would still be on roster."

"In that case," said Carter very quietly, "I shall be forced to bring my own case before the court, with Dr. Levi as my counsellor."

This certainly hit the ball into the opposite court, as Carter was by now a fairly well-known figure to a public who had followed his adventures.

Nate stood up. "Permission to address their lordships."

"So granted."

"Milords, England is a partial theocracy, as you, milord Chancellor, have just described. As long as the Queen is the head of the Church of England, it would make a very interesting case to argue; as such, she can scarcely accept a resignation on the grounds you have just presented, which spring from religious bias. I must admit I would be delighted to argue such a case. Theocracy is one of my pet subjects. It still exists—I am sure we all remember the unfortunate Mr. Rushie."

Then he and Nate watched as the men in front of them realized they had been backed into a corner into which Nate could tie them up for the next decade.

After some murmuring and muttering, the judges appeared to be slowly conceding to Carter's proposal. If they had a big mess now, what would happen if they bounced Carter? It was apparent he would not go quietly, not quietly at all.

"You will remain silent on the situation for six months, absolutely."

"Absolutely."

"At full pay." That would be Nate.

"And likewise for MsT." That would be Carter.

Surrender was imminent.

As they exited the building, there was a crowd and there was media. One reporter ran to meet them with a microphone to ask, "Dr. Levi, how do you feel about this outcome?"

"Young man, I never thought I would live to be so old, so I rarely bought anything new. But given the joy of this day, I am planning to buy a new hat! Perhaps I shall need one!"

He reached up to take it off his head as Carter steadied him, then skimmed it out into the crowd, who responded with a loud cheer, with people jumping to try to catch it where it came down.

CHAPTER 15

One week into his sabbatical, Carter looked ahead to face a blank universe. He rang Mildred Stevenson.

"Mildred—if I may—this is Carter Braxton. I have received as of now several offers from publishers to write a book, which I am going to attempt, but, if you would be so kind, I would covet your advice. I do not necessarily want to go for the highest price, only the one which will do the best job."

"Then I would go for McCabe & Fortuna," she replied.

"Thank you. From now on, it's 'Carter,' as I trust I may have some recourse to your good advice. I have little experience with the literary world."

"Why, certainly, Sir—Carter. I would be thrilled, actually!"

"I realize this is short notice but would you like to diner tonight?"

"What time?"

"Valerie," Carter called. "What time will dinner be ready tonight?"

"Six o'clock, all right? Too early?" It generally was by British standards; however, they ate early to eat with Mercy, who then had time to finish her homework. "Six thirty?"

"OK. Miss Stevenson, is six thirty too early for you?"

"I'll be there."

Next, Carter called the records office of the courts, asking that copies of his write-ups of his cases be delivered. It was a staggering request, but by now the Court perceived how useful MsT. could be.

Promptly at six thirty, Miss Stevenson was at their door. "Let me take your coat," said Valerie; once she had it in hand, she plunged into the hallway closet to find a sturdy hangar for an overcoat, murmuring to herself—

"Now, why do all the ones one wants seem to have disappeared?"

Carter smiled. "If it has to do with wood, leave her at it. "Sherry?

"Lovely."

After an amiable dinner, with Mercy included, Carter asked, before dessert, "Mildred, what do I need to know to write a book?"

"Grab your readers straightaway. I don't think we needs worry about a target audience."

"Could you give me an example of grab straightaway?"

"We have, milord. Guilty. The prisoner will be remanded to the judge for sentencing. Then, of course, one has to choose the right segue—flashback, intermittent memories, so forth. It would be a bit discouraging at first, until you establish style and narrative voice, but after that, I assure you, it will come much more easily. It's like household renovations. It's awful, but they tell you when it's finished, you won't remember the awful part."

"Mildred, would you consider being my editor?"

"Retirement is only a matter of months away and—you know"—she paused, "Well, I am still as keen to run as a greyhound!"

"What shall we do first? Have you got a fax machine at home?"

"Not before I could help it, but I expect 'before' has got to up- anchor now."

"How shall I start?

"Begin with a list of the most influential people in your life."

"Me! Me! Me!" Cried Mercy. "I can read in Hebrew!"

"Thank you, Mercy," Carter said. He took a small sip of bourbon. "Now, Mildred, you can see what it is like to be an overly-bright child!"

"Yes—thank you, young lady," Mildred replied.

Mildred looked at her watch. "I am terribly sorry, but I am an early to bedder —at my age, if I stay up past ten o'clock, I am in a fog all the next day!"

"Let me drive you home."

"Oh, that's not necessary!! Please just call a taxi!" However, Mercy was already jumping up and down again, crying, "Poppy, can I go too? Can I go too?"

"At age nine she will be fresh as a daisy, despite staying up past her bedtime!" So, he backed the Rover out of the garage and the two ladies, one young, one not so young, jumped in.

"What a treat to be driven through London!"

"Good night, Mildred. I shall start on the list tomorrow."

"Yes—do!"

"What a wonderful evening," said Valerie, when the Rover arrived home, while Mercy was hustled into her pyjamas.

CHAPTER 16

"What do you think we have to do about this children of Abraham project?"

That question was one they really not needed to ask themselves after the photograph appeared, for it was answered for them by a storm of letters to the editor, articles, radio and television interviews with 'talking heads' to the effect, pro or con, "Are we really supposed to believe in this, in the twentieth century?" *A big deal for a week or two*—or so Carter thought.

Once the phone rang, it did not stop, and some callers were full of vituperation, threats, outage; others were questioning; others were overflowing with happiness; many were of the opinion "if there were a God there would be no wars, poverty, famine."

Carter had the phone disconnected to install an unlisted number. Someone slashed Carter's automobile tires. One night, someone inserted cloth into an open bottle of whisky, lit it, and then threw it at the house. The neighbor across the street called the fire department, who put out the remaining flames and checked the perimeter of the house carefully.

Next morning, Valerie found three symbols on paper, weighed down by rocks on the lawn. Immediately she faxed them to John Hawkins, who agreed they were hexes, which she burned immediately. She also faxed a copy of them to Carter at the office, lest MsT. open any envelopes containing more of the same, which would be burned.

John had a security plan. It arrived on four feet.

"If we leave a police car outside, it will be obvious. People can find holes in time when they change shifts; or can they see the back of the house. This is King."

Out stepped a huge German shepherd with the usual tan and black markings of the breed, as well as the strange half- crouch of the hind legs, as if he were ready to immediately pounce. He looked about imperially.

"I hope our house is good enough for him!" muttered Carter.

His handler explained the dog usually bonded most closely with one person, asking them to come into the back yard, so he could introduce them to King.

"Would you step up to him with me, Sir Carter?" Then he gave the command to "Protect!" to King, who shook his coat. Next came Valerie, who received the same reaction. Last, came Mercy, who stepped up holding the handler's hand, for to a nine-year-old, King was somewhat overwhelming.

"Hello, Mr. King," she said shyly.

"Protect!"

King wagged his tail, then offered her his paw, all to everyone's astonishment.

"She seems to be the one," said the handler. Then he took them through the list of commands, starting with a simple "sit." The handler asked for Carter's pocket handkerchief, and, moved King around to the side of the house, where he was told, "Stay!" Then Carter's handkerchief was deposited under some fallen leaves; King was told, "Smell!"

Carter noticed the trainer was consulting his watch every few minutes. "Is something wrong?"

"The Shepherds only hold a scent for about twenty minutes—then it gets too mixed in with other smells. If you want a tracker, you need a bloodhound. Those long ears keep the scent fresh."

"Oh, like Toby!"

"I see you are a Sherlock Holmes fan, young lady!"

Last, the handler brought a dummy out of the car and propped it up at the end of the yard. "Hold and bite!" King seized the dummy's leg in an iron grip. The trainer moved back again until the dog, crouching slightly, was ordered to "Attack!"

King gave a leap, sinking his teeth into the dummy's thigh and stomach, then proceeded to shred it completely apart with his teeth.

"Wow!" said Mercy, jumping up and down with excitement.

"Where does he—" Carter began, wanting to know where the dog ought to sleep.

"He can have my extra bed!" said Mercy, who had lost a few playmates with all this commotion. King gave Carter a dirty look. *That dog's not going to like me.*

As for Carter, he had to become accustomed to looking in the rear-view mirror, where two eyes and a big black nose looked back at him; then he gave the command, "Down!"

$$C\ H\ A\ P\ T\ E\ R\quad 17$$

'Having grown up in Clapham, I had always a certain dis-comfort at being where I was not supposed to be. I had never quite realized how strong was the impulse to fit in until I was safehoused. At first I had an urgent desire to have a run along the Embankment, until slowly I realized during that activity I was the reflection of myself others mirrored back to me; they saw me as a successful professional chap runner so I could be assured this is what I was actually was, not some sort of imposter. This self- impression as such was most needed when I was acting as myself rather than as a judge; the former was undecided, whereas the latter was to an extent merely a projection of my function.

'The enforced solitude which was at first so depressing slowly gave way to being able to concentrate on myself rather than the self as others saw me. My social surroundings, where my attention was always given to other people, making sure I was conforming to the expected, was now removed. I could come home, don my pyjamas and if I so desired, open a bottle of ale, then sit down to watch a soccer match, with no need to keep up a side conversation on how the game was going. It was a novel effect to have myself for company. I could talk to myself or to the telly; if I was angry I could shout without alarming any one; I could leave my study the mess I preferred without orders not to disturb anything. I was myself, whoever that was.'

FAX:' Do you want to throw away Clapham?'

FAX: 'You told me one should grab the reader right away—they probably would not juxtapose High Court with Clapham.'

"You can tell your reader what happened to you while you were safehoused, or, you can SHOW them," Mildred responded.

"Yes, I want Clapham. What did you say? Grab 'em at the beginning with something attention getting?"

Valerie tapped gently at his door. "Would you take a look at this and tell me what you think?"

"It's cute—but what is it?"

"Saint Francis scolding the wolf. I made it as funny as I could. First three people in each store which carries our brand gets a free roast beef if they guess."

Carter began to laugh. "You will cause a run on religious bookstores for St. Francis!! I'm afraid I don't know the story line."

"Near a village named Gubbio in Italy, a wolf ate whatever he could find, including people. Francis went out to scold him and to make a deal: people in the village would leave food for him so he wouldn't have to hunt for it any more. Of course, modern scholars poo-poo it as a nice story. Unfortunately, when they took the altar apart at Gubbio— they found the skeleton of a wolf inside it."

"I see!"

"I must go paint it now."

"Then, what happens?"

"I hand deliver it to a company able reproduce it." Off she went.

Now, in his study, Carter could hear Valerie on the house phone, engaged in what appeared to be a disturbing conversation.

"It's simple!" he heard her say firmly. "Just take them off, but put a few aside; someday, they might become collectibles!"

"What is it?"

"There have been complaints about my sticker with St. Francis, enough so, some store managers took the meat off the shelves hoping they will not have to discontinue ordering from us."

"Did I hear you simply tell them to take the stickers off?" His barrister's disturbance gauge was rising.

"You did."

"Why, for Heaven's sake?"

"Because one of the titles for the devil is 'creator of discord.' People are all too used to spiritual dogfights. We shall just wait and see." He disagreed. But she was right.

Several weeks passed without any stickers on the Herrington beef. Then, both Valerie and store managers began to receive letters from an unusual source: mothers whose children were upset that the stickers had been removed, and, moreover, wanted to know what had happened to the wolf. Even notes in crayon in child-like handwriting were delivered to stores. Managers began to ring, asking her what they could do.

"If I did not know the vicious practitioners of trying to rid anything of something of a religious nature, I would say, put stickers on some in one section, no stickers on another. Yet I do not think it would satisfy them."

"Are we giving atheists this much power?" said Carter sceptically. "Studies show they are generally unhappy, so writing frightening letters is an easy outlet. I mean, how many Christopher Hitchens are there after all?"

"No, Carter. There are still pagans in England—very different from atheism."

"Rubbish!"

Valerie took her own action; she hired a secretary, a grey-haired woman who was so sentimental, the notes from children made her cry. Store managers were relieved she had taken it into her own hands, allowing her to put up a poster that if anyone who desired a sticker would send in the price ticket from a Herrington purchase, they would receive the missing sticker back by the following mail, autographed in place of stickum.

At first, only a few shy letters came in. However, when the stickers were returned by mail, children who had heard about this scheme also began to write, with crayons, pencils, paint—perhaps misspelled, perhaps non-grammatical, but all wanting to know what had happened to their wolf, who looked so gentle. Valerie had them all sent a sticker, even if the letter did not include a sticker from their brand of beef.

Managers, Valerie realized, were being in a cross-fire; she proposed that each Saturday she would sit outside one of the stores which carried the Herrington brand, to hand out the stickers in sequence to those who came in person instead of writing. Most managers were happy; she would not be on their property, but would be a marvelous marketing draw! Of course, Mercy would be with her.

At mid-week, the Sidi phone to say he would soon be arriving in London to look into renovating his building for a new and different purpose. After the recent despondent occurrences, this provided an uplift to their spirits!

As Saturday grew nearer, Carter found himself becoming more and more disinclined to spend a day outside a market with a hoard of enthusiastic children. Mercy, who was still most attentive to his every mood, with a tactfulness one hardly expected from a child going ten, asked, "That will be a good day for you to stay home and write, wouldn't it, Poppy? Don't you think so, Mummy?"

"Why—of course," said Valerie, who had fully been expecting Carter to accompany them. Though her heart sunk, and her shadow drew a bit nearer, she could not help but notice a certain look of relief on his face.

"Come on, Mummy," said her child enthusiastically. "We can do it! Come, King!"

The phone rang in his study as he heard the car pull away. "Sidi!" He said, to the well-recognized voice.

"This is not your voice mail? I am not only leaving a message I have arrived?"

"No, no, I am at home writing. Valerie –is…"

"I know where she is," said the Sidi, and hung up.

The two adventurers were happy to find a table set up for them, with pens and pens all with the supermarket logo on them! King vanished under the table. It began slowly, but, as the pace increased, a well-recognized black limousine with darkened windows drew up driven by Khalil, containing the Sidi, who lowered the back window to inquire, "Are you protected?"

He was not prepared for a huge dog to come out from under the table, the skin of his lips pulled back to reveal substantial teeth. Although he was immediately told, "Protect!" The dog raised his paw, appearing ready to jump in the lowered window.

"Very good!" he said quickly, and raised his blackened window. Dogs were a graceless animal in Islam. Pursuit of prey was achieved by hawks.

Mercy dropped to her hands and knees, crawling under the table. "Hug time, King!" she said. (The police trainer who was still working with Mercy and King once a week had initially been stymied that this little girl who wanted to hug her dog). Her arms went around the dog's thick protective neck hair, hands stroking his tan and black coat, cheek against the side of his face, telling him what a good dog he was; King could not resist a few wags of his tail.

A taxi drew up, and Carter, who had been unable to work after the Sidi's phone call, jumped out, calling "Mercy!"

As Mercy crawled out on the pavement, he thought, *Ah, I suspect nearly ten will be the age of skinned knees.*

C H A P T E R   1 8

Mildred had told him it was important to get the first sentence right. Carter experimented with all different beginnings, but in the end, decided to simply stick as close to the truth as possible.

FAX: 'It was a rainy autumn day in 1996 when the judge took his seat at the bench of High Court, Criminal Division. He was breaking in a new wing collar, which rubbed against his neck.'

FAX: 'You are starting out in the third person?'

FAX: 'Recall Olivier's film of Henry V? Small start before great expansion. Have to figure out when to switch to first person.'

FAX: 'I see you have your own style. Stick with it.'

Carter began to write: 'The case which lay before the judge demanded that he would be under twenty-four-hour protection...' and stopped.

Carter turned his opening sentence every which away, but no matter how he re-arranged it, it simply refused to come alive, merely sat there. He closed his eyes. Why couldn't he seem to write? Eventually a silence was reached, and in that silence, he felt a presence behind him. What was it? *It was Norah.*

So that was the deep reason. He had made the mistake of showing his argumentations to Norah, who tore them apart. As much as one might think that did not affect him, there was a silent scar. He did not think of it often, but when he did, it took on the tone of a moral amputation, for he had thought marriage was something that was supposed to fall into place. She was from a good family who were not thrilled with him.

The differences in the backgrounds were wide, even given all his efforts to raise his status. He thought she might admire him for all he had accomplished; instead, he sometimes had the feeling she was looking down on him.

In retrospect she may well have been.

She then delivered the crushing blow of falling in love with someone else. He never wanted to be dumped again. *No entanglements. And a bit of payback taken out on other women, of course.* No one else had ever dumped him; he never let things get to the stage where that could have happened. It was only some years later, reading over one of his ex-wife's barrister cases, he realized that she was using one of his arguments. Unfortunately, she never made it to silks.

Val did ask me for my opinion on St. Francis, in a very innocent and trusting way, and actually seemed to welcome it.

New wine for new wineskins.

Slowly, he began to be able to write some more.

FAX: 'Why, the judge thought, had he decided to break in a new wing collar, which rubbed against his neck, the very same day he first had to wear a bullet proof vest? Was it penitential? For today was also the day of his best friend's funeral.'

FAX: 'Better. Intertwined stories.'

FAX 'Mildred, I've boiled down a trial whose transcript would run far too many pages, just noting the salient parts.'

'The judge,' he continued, 'had taken on—or, more properly, been enlisted—to sit on the bench in a trial which would require total security, including any interaction with friends, which might put them in danger.'

'On this day, at the most important of his judicial career to date, the judge's main concern was to blink back tears. When at last he felt ready, he entered court, to begin the usual procedure of the sheriff announcing the judge, the nature of the case, then asking the Crown barristers to introduce themselves, followed by the defence. The judge gave the usual charge to the jury about the defendant being innocent until being found guilty beyond a reasonable doubt, as well as asking the prosecution if they could see the defendant here present.'

Carter found it relatively easy to flow along with the instalment. 'OK!' he said, smiling to himself, as he wrote the last line of the first chapter. 'The judge stepped forward to meet Sidi el Hassem.'

'I can't recall if he salaamed, then I responded in kind, or if we shook hands,"' he wrote to Mildred.

He faxed it all to Mildred, who never used what she referred to as 'one of those hideous machines that marks up pages with red ink.' She wrote in the margin by hand, while Carter studied a book which demonstrated editorial signs like 'en.'

The fax machine engaged. He jumped up! Out came the pages. He could make out little symbols as it came page by page, but at the end, she had crossed out the business about whether they salaamed or shook hands, which he had thought so very clever. In the margin was the comment, 'too windy.' If you must use it then start with 'I do not remember.'

Carter could not help it, he had to show it to his wife. "I take it that 'I do not remember' may be too vague," she said. "Wouldn't you have known you were supposed to return a salaam at that time?"

"How?"

"What did you think of the Sidi when you first met him?"

"His aura seemed to permeate the whole room."

"Good!"

Out went shaking hands or salaaming.

He continued.

'Despite the judge's best efforts, his attention wavered at first between the evidence being presented in front of him, and mental pictures that flashed through his mind of a church service in a building of which he had clear mental picture, then the procession to the family cemetery in a natural clearing about a hundred yards beyond a house, where the sun fell through the leaves to the ground like lace; then, that slow letting down of the coffin by ropes ever so gently looped beneath it by Pendragon men standing on boards placed across the hole dug for the grave, until the coffin finally settled on the bottom.'

'Then, the cursory handfuls of dirt or flowers into the grave, after which, it was traditional for the mourners to leave the professionals to fill in the grave and place the tombstone. The judge could not imagine that at this point, the eldest child would not dismiss the hearse, so he, as well as their workers, could fill in the grave by themselves. He should have been one of them, tucking his friend into his final resting place.'

'His friend was no more. He must move ahead, relying more and more on just himself. His attention slowly returned to the Crown's opening statement—a 'dream team,' as the Americans called it, of course, one which could only be assembled by man of means. Yet the defence was equally formidable: for the corporations which had been defrauded of crude oil were just as able to pay top silks; but the Sidi's documentation was voluminous and undebatable.'

'His appointment to a judgeship had been three years ago; not really time to develop the depth and wisdom usually expected in the making of a judge, except for his old professor's constant training during this period of time.'

'The judge's mind moved back to the trial. He could see the defence team's delight in having a "raw" judge, circling around him like sharks anticipating a juicy piece of raw meat.'

'All is ready, milord,' the usher told the judge. Everyone stood when the judge entered the room from his chambers, made a short bow, then, everyone but the defendant sat down.'

'The clerk of court announced the case, then asked Sanderson to state his name and address.'

'Ian Sanderson, Elean Aegeis island, Beauly River, Scotland.'

'Would you translate that for the jury?'

'Eagle Island, Beauly River, Scotland.'

'How do you plead?'

"Not guilty."

Well, of course you do, or we wouldn't all be here, thought then judge.

'Does the Crown council desire to present evidence gathered which may include some terminology with which the jury is unfamiliar?'

'We would, milord.'

'The prosecution barrister rose to address the jury. They had received permission to project a map onto a screen, because the evidence covered so much territory.'

'The case before the Crown involves crude oil theft, commonly known as 'bunkering.'

'This practice can be carried on above ground if the pipeline passes over sectors of earth, or under water, if it passes under water. Holes are pierced in the pipeline; the particular pipeline in question is one which runs from Norway to Nigeria, and is now owned by Shell Oil,' said the prosecutor, carefully picking up the transparency of the pipeline, then wrapping it in preservative material for the clerk of courts, who labelled it as Exhibit A.'

'Now, crude oil has two uses; it can be used in its original form to make products such as blacktop, or, it can be refined to make it into petrol or other refined oil products. In order for the latter, there must be a mediator between the seller and the refiners, and, because such a mediator was discovered to live within the confines of the United Kingdom, it was decided to try him within the jurisdiction of London.'

'With your lordship's permission, we would like to present a list of offenses to the clerk of court, as to read them out would take an undue amount of time.'

'So granted.' This, too, went up on the screen.'

'I now call the Crown to proceed its case. Is the Crown ready to call the first witness?'''

'We are, milord. We will now call Sidi el Hassem.'

'There was silence in the court as the usher escorted the Sidi to the witness stand. The judge wondered what the jury expected—a short, ethnically dressed, darker faced man anxious at being in a British court of law, while the judge estimated the Sidi was about six foot in height, still with the carriage of a former Sandhurst cadet, which made him more imposing still. He was wearing the same double-breasted suit he had worn at the Savoy for tea, worn enough as to be comfortable, rather than because of poverty, for he also wore a splendid necktie which was obviously expensive, as were his belt and shoes.'

'Do you swear?' The court presented him with a Koran.'

'I do.'

'Now Mr. el-Hassem…'

'The Sidi raised a hand to summon the prosecutor. 'If I may interrupt the honorable gentleman for a point of clarification,' said the Sidi. 'The correct way to address me is Sidi.'

'It is an honorific title, comparable to your British milord,' announced the prosecutor.'

'So noted. Sidi, please tell us the events which led to your capture of Mr. Sanderson on charges of grand theft and international trade dealings in crude oil?'

'Certainly. We simply began by measuring the volume of crude which left the pipeline in Nigeria against the crude that arrived in Norway; it became clearly evident that a certain volume was being lost or pirated en route. We began to measure the volume of crude as it flowed from point to point on the pipeline, to determine where the largest volumes of crude were being bunkered, then began to investigate these areas intensely, mainly at night, using the usual equipment for nocturnal vision, as well as cameras and video equipment, and extracting sample of crude, using fractioning distillation to keep check on the composition of it, for it can be doctored. I've heard one chap quoted as saying, 'It's black—they won't know the difference.'

'Milord,'said the defence, 'May I interrupt my learnèd friend?'

''Is there a good reason?'

'How can we know what equipment and mechanisms were used to accomplish this?'

'I think it can be deduced *sub silentio,* unless we plan a visit to a construction site,' said the judge. It was a term which meant discerned by implication. 'Are the photographs, charts, and other paperwork available?'

''They are; we have boxed them, bringing one sample box to court.' An usher staggered down to the clerk of court under the weight of a heavy box. 'Please mark this Exhibit B.'

'Would you kindly tell us your next steps?'

'Certainly. We began to separate the volume of crude at given points, to ascertain how much of it had been taken from point to point, which appeared to proceed via land or sea to its destination. These other, missing portions of crude, however, seemed destined for shipment to refineries, in which case, deals were obviously made by someone who was in touch with both the bunkers and the refineries; so at some point, a deal must have been made by a middleman who could effect that exchange, as well as broker prices between buyers and sellers. For reasons of international security, I cannot divulge what equipment used to note the various points where these exchanges of money were made; for our defendant was very meticulous, always changing the points where they were transacted, in cash, usually in in United States dollars; we have several pictures of such transactions, as Mr. Sanderson preferred to make them outside of buildings.'

'We noticed a pattern; the defendant would leave his home in Scotland precisely in time to reach the broker point; although sometimes he would verify his *modus operendi* by, say, taking a small vacation trip to vary the pattern. We have a photographic record of one such diversion; he left Scotland to enjoy a few days of skiing at Gstaad, then continued on to his destination. The timing was always very precise. Also, you will note we used equipment that stamped the date on the photographs automatically; nothing has been written by hand, nor changed by complex technology.'

'When you had gathered this information, what did you do with it?'

'We turned it over to the intelligence services of the relevant states. They took action on it as they chose.'

"How was Mr. Sanderson captured?'

'The intelligence service of the United Kingdom, acting on our timetable, arrested Mr. Sanderson as he attempted to leave the country on a flight from Heathrow to make one of his usual exchanges.'

'Thank you, Sidi. Does the defence wish to cross examine the witness?'

'Milord, we do. Sidi, have you ever been to Nigeria?'

Before the prosecution could object with a relevance, he answered, 'Many times.'

'The judge thought that Sidi had seen an *ad hominem* coming—wealthy man oblivious to poor surroundings.'

'Would you mind telling us what you perceive the condition of the state to be in?'

'Objection.'

'Milord,' said Sidi to the judge, 'I would not be answering without prior knowledge.'

'Proceed.'

'You will recall the collapse in Ghana when the communist government was installed, or the Ivory Coast after the French left, tearing up all the railroad tracks to bring them back to France? Would you care to tell the jury what you think is the cause of this deterioration?'

'Objection! Pure speculation! Leading the witness!'

'Would you say the rise and fall of oil prices has any bearing on the situation?'

'The defence continued as far as it could with this last question.'

'The judge said, 'This is not an examination into international politics. The defence will immediately cease asking irrelevant questions.'

'Yes, milord.'

'You will tell the jury why you have proceeded with this line of questioning.'

'Simply that one end of the pipeline leads into this country.''

'I hope you do not plan to do the same for Norway.'

'The judge should have no worries on this instance.'

'There was a salient pause as the defence barrister turned pages in his notebook. The he asked, 'The witness has made mention of some tracking device which was used. Would this imply the witness is not, as he portrays himself, a free agent, but connected to some governments?''

The judge recalled a sentence written by an American judge: 'the linchpin of your argument is also its Achilles heel.' Here it comes.

'The judge looked at his notes. 'I understand this tracking device is classified material. The law on this is clear: no disclosure of classified information shall be made to a jury in an open trial. As far as being in the pay of various foreign governments, I would entertain proof on that subject if you have any.'

'From the corner of his eye, the judge saw Sanderson smirk, having just seen the law waltz his case into the area of reasonable doubt.'

'After letting silence reign for a portentous moment or two, the judge added, 'However, since there are areas where the law intersects with intelligence, I am obliged to call a recess until legal and intelligence sources have looked into this further, as we have temporarily run into a brick wall.' *No more smile from Sanderson....*

'Generally," 'the judge said,' "No witnesses can be added to the trial lists; however, in this case, an expert witness may be called for. I shall call for recess until we rule on the matter.'

'He turned to the jury. 'Before you step away, the jury will please remain in the vicinity of the court'.

'The trial had been made as open as possible, because it had affected numerous countries in small or large ways, all of whom had been invited to seat intelligence observers in the spectator section, so there would be no hint of deals made in smoke filled rooms. They had all sent a representative, perhaps more, who were not identified to the judge, as, since he was facing them, it was thought it might distract him. Now, that had turned out to be either more convenient or more complicated, depending on the cooperativeness of the various representatives.'

'As they exited separately and arrived separately at the LCD (the Lord Chamberlain's Division), the judge noted, as he took his seat, several of those present, now that he had removed his wig, seemed a bit non-plussed by his youthful lack of grey hair. So, he expected, this must fit a rumor gone around that the judge would be a British 'wunderkind', the judge noted one or two of the men at the table scrutinizing him carefully to see if perhaps he dyed his sideburns.'

'Why the hell didn't you coach...' an American accent burst forth.'

"Gentleman, kindly introduce yourselves and your government connections before you speak.'The judge's tone was carefully polite, restrained.'

'Peter Flemming, United States, Central Intelligence Agency.'

'Mr. Flemming,' said the judge, 'The mores of the first prosecution witness would cause him to tell the whole truth if he so swore without any coaching. The Sidi was a volunteer helping NASA to develop a project, of his own free will, with full understanding this meant the United States entitled him to no favors, for he bankrolls his own operations. I can vouch for that, even if it means a rare device like putting me on the stand. In that case, he is owed especial thanks for working on our calendar; the Islamic calendar moves ahead about ten days every year.'

'The judge appreciated the rather complex, two dial wrist watch which the witness wore.'

"Piers Magnuson, Denmark—Would that time differentiation be able to raise any sort of question?'

'The judge replied he very much doubted it, as basing time by lunar movement was as natural to Islam as was the degree of movement of magnetic north some several dozen degrees each year from Alaska toward Russia was, for their own part of the world. He added that he was sure they were all aware of the years of time it took, first to locate Mr. Sanderson, then to track the various refineries in different countries willing to work with him for a period of time.'

'This particularly effected the United States because of the situation of its southern border with easy access to the Gulf of Mexico. (Here the judge looked intently at Mr. Flemming).'*A real pro. He didn't even twitch.*

'Having identified the rogue refiners is only the first step in convicting them,' the judge opined. 'But it is also possible it may cause some of these refineries to call off if they realize that they are being "tracked," so it can be a double-edged sword. Permission from other countries to concur they also had allowed tracking volunteers to act within their borders might—only might, he added, make the witness's classified intelligence more substantive.'

'In the judge's opinion, without some disclosure permission from NASA, there was no assurance Sanderson's lawyers might find a way to slip through their fingers. He realized this would take communication between the United States intelligence representative and NASA, so he would adjourn back to the courtroom to dismiss the jury until further notice.'

'There was the general noise of abandoning chairs, donning of raincoats, and exits from the conference room. The judge was walking down the corridor when he heard Flemming behind him, calling, 'Judge! Sir! Milord!' running to catch up with him, waving a newspaper.'

'I turned around. Flemming was closing in on me, enough so that I could notice he was wearing cowboy boots, and speaking with a Texas accent.'

'Look at this!' cried Flemming. "It just came over from the office!'

'It was today's copy of the New York Times, with a front page article, 'NASA OK's use of Global Positioning System for U.S. Army.'

'Proof! Proof!' Cried Flemming.'

'Indeed it was. Bob's your uncle. QED!'

'Even a dream team would not wish to take on NASA.'

CHAPTER 19

Carter made the mistake of asking his driver to pass by the Court, and a thin young man who almost blended into the building came up to him.

"Judge Braxton—may I speak with you?"

"If you must."

"My name is Philip Bannerman and I am a first -year barrister. However, to be blunt, my wife and I have a problem which someone told us your wife might be able to help solve."

"What is it?"

"There is a –presence in the house. Not an altogether pleasant one. It makes strange things happen."

"I see. I will ask my wife about it. Do you have a card?"

"They won't be ready until next week."

"Then write your telephone number on the back of one of mine."

When he told Valerie, she responded, "They've got a poltergeist. The poor souls!"

"Would they be upset if we visited them?"

"I don't think so!"

"Let's ring them." The upshot was come soon! sooner! soonest! the better.

The Bannermans lived in a modest flat, one befitting a beginning barrister; as she looked around, Valerie saw that Mrs. Bannerman was a woman of modest height and brown hair, also a tasteful patron of flea markets.

As soon as Valerie stepped into the flat, she experienced a sense of dread. The family appeared exhausted. "Have you been arguing more than usual lately?" Valerie asked.

"Oh, yes!" Mrs. Bannerman burst out. "It's some kind of rage, because *I* don't feel angry at that moment!"

"What else has been happening?"

"Doors and windows open and shut by themselves. The furniture is moved. Things fall but don't break, other things disappear! Sometimes it sounds as if the boiler is exploding!"

She got up to put on a sweater, yet Valerie stopped her. "It won't do any good," she said. "The only way I've ever felt to combat that sort of drop in temperature is a hot bathtub."

"And poor Andy! Something wakes him at three o'clock at night, so he runs into our room and begs to climb into bed with us! Even when he comes home from school, if no one is here, he will sit on the steps until I come home."

"The television goes on and off," Andy added.

"Sometimes we hear something like claws scratching on the wood floor."

"Let me read you short list of phenomena given to me as a child: noises made by a poltergeist; noises of dishes in the kitchen, noises on the steps, noises in the television set despite it not working, the faucet turns on and off by itself as do lamps, hearing disembodied voices, feeling a strange presence around, hearing of being called by name, seeing rapid passing shadows, appearance of small or large bruises on the body with no pain, seeing human shapes or ghosts. You can see it is a subject which has been well-studied, and produces the same symptoms. I hope that will be reassuring."

So that was in that battered school notebook Valerie always carried with her, though he gave it little thought—probably friends' addresses, or some such.

"Tell me—is Andy in the room alone at these times?"

"Why—yes!"

"Don't let that happen. Poltergeists prefer their victims to be young, the younger, the better."

"But it's quiet as a mouse just now!

"Does Andy develop unaccounted bruises with no pain?"

"Why did you ask?"

"Because I have been developing a facsimile since Carter told me about it this morning. Tell me, Andy, do you have a bruise on your thigh?"

"Yes, Ma'am."

Carter had wondered how Valerie developed bruises she could not account for, which indeed, she said, did not hurt her.

"But it's quiet as a mouse! How can you believe us?"

"It knows you have visitors. We'll have to provoke it."

Diving into her purse, she drew out her Bible and a cross. Standing in the middle of the room, she held up her cross, commanding, "Spirit, in the name of Jesus Christ, manifest yourself in some way. Spirit, give me your name."

Instantly, a cacophony of the noises the Bannermans had told her about began to occur; doors opened and shut, drawers did the same; windows opened and closed. Andy began to cry.

"Why don't you take Andy outside into the backyard for some fresh air?"

Mrs. Bannerman was only too happy to comply. They had just begun to discuss the situation when she reappeared.

"I thought you were taking him out," said her husband.

"But I saw you at the back window motioning me to come in."

"No! We were all right here!"

"So—," said Valerie slowly, "It materialized in a shape which resembled your wife."

"It must have! It was shaped just like her!" Added her husband.

"Oh, yes, I rather fancy sometimes they like to be tricky."

"But—how do we get rid of it?"

"Prayer." Windows slammed shut.

"Oh, no! Not in this house!"

"My wife is an atheist."

"Oh, I see! In that case I'm afraid there is little I could do for you. In fact, your lack of belief is the probable cause this thing to choose your flat as its habitation. I'm so sorry."

Valerie gathered her pocket book, then her husband helped her on with her coat. The door closed behind them.

CHAPTER 20

"Now, I needs only clear one thing from my docket before I sit down, pen in hand, Valerie."

"Such as?"

"You once said you believed there was a reason I had such difficulty with the atonement. Now is the time to tell me why."

"I was hoping to get a picture of your family's spiritual connections—on both sides."

"What spiritual connections?" he snorted.

"That's just the point!"

Carter pondered. "I think the only real way is to tackle my father. He is retired now; since then, from what I hear, he mostly sits watching the telly, drinking ale. I will not ring ahead, he will put me off, so we must perform an assault. Valerie, it is going to be ugly— he is dying of alcoholic poisoning. Tomorrow it is, then." Carter wound through streets Valerie did not even know existed, until he stopped at a small, run-down going- to -ruin house, a no-hoper, badly in need of paint as well as repairs. Carter pulled out a key and unlocked the door.

"Who the hell are you? Looks as if you made a wrong turn."

"No, I am afraid not. I am your son Carter, this is my wife, Valerie. May we come in?" Since it was apparent Carter was not going to take 'no' for an answer, his father grunted. He was still seated in a chair that smelled of urine and feces.

"Take a seat, Valerie, one won't be offered." But Valerie was wandering thoughtfully toward one of the windows.

"Wot's the matter—not classy enough for you?"

"I was noting that your muntins are so brittle they will collapse shortly, leaving the glass—that is, the lights—to fall out." She pressed on one of the pieces of wood until the end cracked off.

"Well, wot do you want aside from telling me that me house is falling apart?"

"My family is in the wood business. We could have it fixed for you."

"I don't want no charity!"

"Unfortunately for both of us, Mr. Braxton, it appears it is not charity, but family."

"Wot?"

"It seems to have escaped your notice that you have acquired another daughter-in-law, while I have acquired you, whether each of us like it or not!" exclaimed Valerie with some heat.

"I'm sure, since you have missed all the other events in my life, my wife is no interest to you!" Carter added.

"Here is the family business card, should you relent to your obliviousness before the windows fall in."

"D'you know what kind of bastard you've married? He took my wife away from me!"

"So I've heard," said Valerie drily, "since you were working her to death. I am proud to know he saved her from a most unpleasant situation."

"Mum said at times when you were drunk you would say you wished you were a better man. But wishing never makes things happen."

"Is that so? That what they taught you at Oxford?"

"Oh, I learned that here."

"Is that a knock in the wall?" Valerie asked.

"Oh, ya, I get it all the time—probably the house falling down."

"How long has that been going on?" She looked at Carter. "Is it since his wife died?"

"I dunno." The old man answered her.

"She was a good woman. I think she acted as a shield," said Carter abruptly. "That period of my life after she died did feel strangely like a compulsion."

"It was," said his wife. "These—beings that are knocking can infest people."

Once outside, she said, "You had a narrow escape, thank God. Anything occult will block belief in original sin and atonement, Carter, and with your mother gone, it could truly settle on you. God knows, there were plenty of cultural influences that negate belief in these articles of faith, like George Bernard Shaw, for example, who negated the atonement by calling it the religion of the gibbet, and so on. Thank God, He overcame it in you."

C H A P T E R   2 1

Carter put another trial introduction on his desk, then began to write. 'The minute I entered the safety of my office, the dread passed. It would come again when I was driven back to my safehouse, yet leave again once I was there.

'I removed every item of my judge's regalia with reverence, for I never knew when the day might come I would never see them again. In went my horsehair wig to its blue and red box; then the wing collar into its box, my bands in their case, my black stole and waist wrap, last, my red silk summer gown.'

Then he stopped. What had he felt next, what had happened next? Was this a good addition? *I have written countless pages for court case reports, but not one of them ever included the pronoun 'I.'*

Then he made his list.

Mother

Valerie

Tony

Nate and Debora

Adrian and his family

John

Sidi

Khalil

It was not a long list. He went to bed.

In the morning, the phone rang. "Carter? I have a courier on the way—send it over!"

"But all I've written is a list!"

"It's important to get started. I don't want you to freeze on me, to write one hundred opening paragraphs, and unable to decide on which one!! As you know, my fax is not working yet."

"Yes, ma'am!" The courier came, the courier went, and then several hours later, Mildred called.

"Must I start with my mother?"

"Yes, *ab initio*."

Carter felt tears come to his eyes while he choked up. He had to clear his throat several times. "My mother was a remarkable woman. She made me into what I am today. She was not frightened, nor did she scorn my prodigy profile; she helped it along, so when neighborhood people used to mock her for thinking she'd have a son who would go to university, she would look them in the eye and say, 'That's right.' She was a nice girl in an environment where most girls were not so nice, which is what attracted my father's notice, I suspect. A nice girl who would work herself to death without complaint.

"He was rather handsome then, while he could turn on charm the way one turns on a faucet. He swept her off her feet, then, they married, when he turned back into the surly brute he was. She held a full-time job, did the cooking, cleaning, laundry—oh, he got full usage out of her, while I tried to make little interventions such as reading her the newspaper in a crazy fashion; I also hung out the laundry. Father and my brother Bert were virtually identical in their attitude towards her.

"It appears she talked to the boss about my idea about her pension when I was very young, because she quoted me as saying "Mummy," so her boss had found a way to save her money. We decided put AVR into her pension plan—that is extra money, beyond what was owed,—so she could retire early.

"We got hold of a solicitor who told us how to take it out if she retired early, but, as her heart was weakening, she did have cause; I wanted to book her into a cushy nursing home, but she wanted to be near her friends—private room, no cooking, cleaning, working—free to go out and walk about—shop, go to the movies, visit with her never- a -very -welcome family at our house.

"I was so happy I had been able to repay Mum —if only slightly! We could phone, then Saturdays, we visited, we could take in a show or a movie of an evening; she did not want to travel, she would always tell me 'I hate to pack, dear!' when she died, then a door seemed to swing shut on memories—perhaps it was just too painful or traumatic—where has that young man gone, Mildred? I think Valerie has just told me where."

Mildred faxed back, 'develop this more.'

CHAPTER 22

"It's time to visit the publisher to sign a contract. I am going to be your agent – I read every clause three times. Meet me there in an hour?" It was Mildred.

"Yes, ma'am!"

The building was not excessive; good brick, then, as one got closer, one noticed a frieze over the door: whoever was within had a good sense of humor—carved into it was a large fish with a boot disappearing down its mouth, and a squatting monkey ready to crap on one's head. To finish it off, a lion was bending down with open jaws, ready to eat all ye who enter here.

"Like it?" asked Mildred.

"Love it."

On the top floor was the requisite glass windows which formed the walls, an imposing desk, a president behind it. "Why—Mildred! So –surprised to see you!"

"I will be acting as Sir Carter's agent."

"Oh, mercy me!" said the president, rolling his eyes. "Here's the contract. Pull up a chair."

Mildred began to make the occasional little question mark; at one point, she scribbled a large X . The president went quietly about his business. Carter, to use one of his brother-in-law Buddy's phrases, just kicked back.

"This film clause won't do. Any rights to be sold to a British company? You know we'd get a lot more in America. Let anyone have a purchase bid, on understanding it will be outsourced to a British film company."

The president sighed. "The contract will have to be re-written."

"Then re-write it, Tom; whilst you're at it, I've made a few small corrections."

Outside, she smiled at Carter, saying, "Let 'em know you're going to box their ears as soon as you come out the gate. They always think they can toss a lady."

"We shall have to return another day."

"Oh, no, they have some speed typists there. Let's go have a nice lunch."

Carter had a beer, while Mildred returned to her ladylike self, took off her gloves, and ordered a sherry. "You see, one has to be scrappy sometimes at times like this. They did swallow my change in the film clause."

"A film? Doesn't that stretch credibility?"

"It's simply prudent to cover all your wickets."

"Are you sure you're not a barrister? By the way, what per cent does an agent take?"

"Ten per cent."

Carter knew this was a low-ball figure, but that he'd have to move carefully, not making too big a jump. "Fifteen?"

"Done." She laughed. "It's so very interesting. I'd have done it for nothing!"

"I wouldn't. What's that phrase—the laborer is worth her hire? Something like that."

Mildred's mobile poked her discreetly. She went into the restroom to answer it. Meanwhile, Carter summoned the waiter, who nodded, bringing over the bill.

Carter had just taken his credit card out of his wallet when Mildred came charging over, grasped the card, and said to the waiter, "Just put it on my bill!"

"Yes, ma'am, Miss Stevenson!"

"Ah," she said philosophically as she sat down, "I expect I shall miss an expense account."

Nice to be treated to lunch by a lady. Two ladies. Valerie and Mildred.

CHAPTER 23

A formal letter in vellum with the return address of the Archbishop of Canterbury arrived, stating that a common meeting would be gratefully considered a matter of propriety, emphasizing that it was understood the Sidi would be bringing x-rays of the man who was alleged to be healed.

"X rays? Now why would I wish to do that? I know that I am healed."

"Because an such an invitation is a considered high honor in jolly old England, Sidi!"

"Why should I care about what this man thinks about what kind of honor he is extending to me? He is not my spiritual leader. I have not come to talk to sceptics.

"I have my own building, my own transportation system for those I wish to invite. I am seeking the Russian Orthodox community at Walsingham as well as some Eastern Orthodox on the Isle of Man I have heard still exist, then, after that, the word of mouth, as I do not know where to look further. I shall invite the Archbishop, but with this understanding: this event is under our control.

"Now," said the Sidi, "we must be correct and send the first ecclesiastical invitation to Pope Tawadros of the Coptic Orthodox Church. I will have to procure a scribe to write it in elegant Arabic, for his title is very long, and the wording should be extremely carefully thought out.

"First off," Sidi continued, "I will find a scribe tomorrow, to dictate a letter to the Pope, asking if he would honor us with his presence; I will have it flown to him in Cairo. Until I receive a reply, I will not correspond with any of the English clergy as I wish to make sure Tawadros may wish to come; we can ever-so-tactfully convey he would lead a hierarchical line-up."

"His title is Pope?"

"Yes, dear Valerie, he was given that title at least three centuries before the Pope at Rome—a fact the Vatican acknowledges. St. Mark, you know, was martyred in Alexandria. However, the point is, the Pope is always a monk, so I do not know what type of transportation he would prefer. There is first class airline, there is the Gulfstream— it is too long a trip by helicopter. Pardon me."

He rang Khalil by mobile and a long conversation ensued in Arabic. When he rang off, the Sidi laughed. "Hussein's leg is healing well."

"I'm sorry we don't have a letterhead," said Valerie.

"Then we will do it by the day after tomorrow," replied the Sidi. He had brought a kettle to place on the top plate of their cooker; he liked to hear the sound of the kettle loudly whistle, so, he did not use their electric kettle. Desert sheikhs or commoners alike would dismount their camels to cook a pot of tea over camel dung; this explained his preference. While he was standing by the stove, his mobile rang, he slipped into Arabic, chattering away, his hosts discerned, with his family.

"Do you think he does this every night?"

"When they have the same time window!"

This was a side of the Sidi they had never seen; a smile was on his face, a cup of sweet tea in his hands, and a sigh of content. It was fascinating to note that a figure with all the Sidi's charisma had a private face.

After he rang off, he told them, with a smile, "In short—in very short—Khalil is scared stiff at the idea of flying the Pope by himself, so he has enlisted Danilya and Hanan as his hospitality team.

They would like to come to London—they will be with us tomorrow! They will stay overnight, then fly the scroll to Tawadros."

C H A P T E R   2 4

As they sat at Farnborough, waiting for Khalil and his wives, they could not help but think back over the events which had had so much impact on all their lives.

It all began one evening several years ago, when Khalil had called Carter and told him that he had some news that he would prefer to tell him in person, could he meet him at Farnborough the next day? Of course, his friend had agreed.

Khalil's face had darkened that fateful day.

"Honorable Judge, prepare yourself for some unfortunate news. In one village, Sidi was stoned, as he was traveling with infidels without converting them. Very fortunately, they were merely throwing stones rather than capturing him to put him in sand. We had insisted Sidi wear his Nomad badge and give us his word of honor he would not dispose of it. He would have been furious, certainly, but we had backup about ten miles behind him, for these sects of Muslim faith are very volatile.

"One day the waves emanating from him were erratic, so we sent a chopper to a village whose people were still throwing rocks. The pilot settled down in front of the pile of rocks, keeping the rotor blades running so no one dared approach. Our men feared the worst as they dug through the rubble. He was still alive, but badly injured. We immediately sent for Mohammed and his assistant Amal with our medicated chopper, which arrived almost immediately. Now some people had discovered how to throw rocks under the rotor blades, so I picked up my automatic rifle and made a line in the sand with bullets, telling them that anyone who threw a rock that over that line would be shot. Mohammed insisted he be lifted on a stretcher with a neck brace. Sidi was very pale, yet was motioning me to put my ear to his lips, which I did trembling, dreading these might be his last words. He whispered, "Cancel my credit cards!"

"But you have no credit cards!"

"Don't be stupid!" Mohammed told me as he bent over Sidi. "Some places won't even take *money* anymore."

Sidi interrupted and gave orders for his two companions to be rescued by the initial helicopter, as our medivac took off, with me as its pilot.

Sidi, can you move your legs?"

"Very little. It is my spine."

Mohammed continued to look troubled. "Ribs?" Sidi nodded. "Amal, bring me that x ray machine." He surveyed the Sidi's midbody. "Ah. Very bad! At least four broken ribs!" He took the Sidi's vital signs, his face showing more and more concern. "Ah! Not good! Something internal! Get that IV into his left arm, Amal, and leave the blood pressure cuff in place!"

"What is it?" I asked.

"It is possible the ribs have pushed inward and torn his liver. I do not have the equipment here to find out, but we may be looking at peritonitis."

"How can we find out?"

"I would have to make an explanatory incision. I'm afraid it is our only chance, even though we have no general anaesthetics."

"Then give me a local."

"Bring me some morphine. Let me get sterile."

"Mohammed pulled on his scrubs and gloves, and Amal tied his facemask; then he injected almost all the local anaesthetic we had into Sidi. Mohammed drew a line with a pen where he wanted to make his incision, right at the umbilicus, as he pronounced it.

"Now I had my back to the operation, so I could only hear. Sidi made a little joke about the upcoming millennium. He said later he learned to joke on the operating table from Ronald Reagan. Then I heard Mohammed say "scalpel," to his assistant as he sucked in his breath and held it to make his hand as steady as possible. Then I heard a long, slow, exhalation. "Praise be his name," said Mohammed, adding that he thought we could make sufficient improvised repairs to get to the hospital.

"My fingers were shaking slightly, so I beseeched Allah for calmness and focus; then a mysterious, unseeable aura began to unfold into my inner eye, like sunrise in the morning, slowly, steadily. We were an invisible speck with the huge blue of sky above us and the sand below. Events were completely out of our control. But what held us in this invisible ocean, the sky? Some power was all about us, which would continue on long after we had died, yet was here long before we were born. In some sense, what was happening was inconsequential. Slowly I became calm."

"It sounds as if you touched eternity," Valerie had said.

"Behind me, I had little except the word, "clamps," which gave me chills."

"Where is the best nearby hospital?" The Sidi asked Mohammed.

"Riyadh," Mohammed replied, "I want the smoothest ride possible. Heading is for the military hospital at Riyadh. Khalil, patch me through to the Emergency section."

"Ask for Dr. Singh," said Sidi weakly. Of course, he *would* have a connection there. "It has a good emergency department. Contact them." It was not as if he had never been wounded before. Sidi might be half dead but he was still in charge!

"Push me up so I can reach the receiver. You will probably have to patch us through."

Mohammed said firmly, "You are my leader, but I am your doctor. Use your head, we are on an airplane; this table has no wheels. I have done the best I can under the circumstances, but we are *not* in a hospital. If you move—and you will move if you wish to transmit—you may tear something loose or contaminate the incision site, or move a clamp. I am beginning to wish I *had* a general anaesthetic!"

"Ask for Doctor Singh," the Sidi repeated. Of course, he would have a contact there—he had one everywhere. I patched us through, while Mohammed stood by, ready to talk to Dr. Singh.

"Give me your bearings." It was Dr. Singh. I did so. "You are about fifty miles out. Put your doctor on. What is your situation?" he asked Mohammed.

"Five broken ribs, a tear in the right liver lobe, vena cava intact, praise be, bile duct holding, several small veins under the liver detached but clamped, possible partial paralysis. I am worried about our IV supply."

"Slow the drip a bit. Keep coming. You'll make it. We are already standing by at the medipad."

"They will have an emergency team ready when we arrive," Mohammed said. Sure enough, when I landed, they unloaded him right onto a gurney and whisked him away, right to the operating room. Here they had all the scanning technology to survey the situation, but there was no need, as surgery had already opened the pathway to the liver.

After they had salaamed each other, Dr. Singh told Mohammed he had done very well in this emergency just by keeping the Sidi alive, let alone effect some surgical repairs.

"We will reconnect the two veins which have torn away—you did the right thing to merely clamp them, it is too fine a surgery to repair under your conditions." When he finished operating, Dr. Singh came over to Mohammed, who was sitting on a couch, holding his head between his hands in a state of semi-shock.

"You did remarkably well," said Dr. Singh.

"That was always my worst nightmare, having Sidi's life in my hands. It was not just I: Allah, praise be to his name, protected him." Mohammed was shaking.

"Yes, doctor, I have been in your position," said Dr. Singh drily. It was a small medical society that Sidi el Hassem allowed to treat him.

"But the worst is not over. "

"What do you mean?"

"I must convince Sidi it is wise to take a painkiller with broken ribs. It will speed the healing process."

Mohammed paused for a moment. Finally he repeated, "It was not just I: Allah, praise be to his name, protected him."

"Is that your opinion, doctor?" Doctor Singh asked with a smile.

"It is."

CHAPTER 25

It was hard to conceive of such a significant man as the Sidi becoming partially paralyzed in his legs: it was from the stone that had hit his spine. It was hard to imagine what it must be like for him, what it must look like. At first it was even difficult to think what to say to him on the telephone. Least embarrassed was the Sidi, and, in time, he invited us to visit him. Of course they could not say no.

Mercy and King would stay behind with Pan.

On the appointed day, they went to Farnborough, to await Khalil, who would whisk them away to an unknown land of theArabian Nights.

Khalil was a popular man at Farnborough; he always brought treats, besides maintaining a friendly manner. In a world in which people with private aircraft were important enough to view the rest of the world as their flunkies, Khalil maintained the philosophy that one should treat the people you met on the way up well, for one might need them on the way down. He had promised friends in the tower he was bringing a surprise, so they kept scanning the skies to see what it might be.

As soon as a dot appeared on the horizon, all the binoculars in the control tower were trained on it.

"Good Lord! I think it's an old Boeing 707! Where the deuce did Khalil get that old crate?"

"Heaven only knows." Carter replied.

The aircraft circled once to view the landing strip; a glint of sunlight hit the wing as if it were winking at them. Then, the pilot, coming in from the south, set it down right at the end of the runway; braking vigorously, stopping almost at the tower, tires smoking. The bystanders cheered.

A figure appeared in the doorway, wearing a black robe, embroidered and beaded from neck to waist, the remainder falling to her ankles, and a head shawl with heavily embroidered edging to which was attached by a chain a crystal beaded face mask. Only her eyes were visible; lights glistened over the crystals, which reached down from the top of her nose to cover the lower section of her face. Before she took a step down the ladder, she put on a cloak which was black with gold piping. Walking toward Carter and Valerie, she held out a hand.

"Welcome, Sir Carter and Lady Valerie. I am Hanan bin Zaid, the younger sister of Khalil's two wives. This is called the sororal form of marriage. Please follow me, we shall go aboard."

Once inside, she removed the chain which her face covering was suspended from her head to her head dress, placing the mask on a seat. When she removed her head dress, her hair was groomed into a perfectly modern style. "I do not wish to be photographed," she told them. Ah, security, was always necessary.

Once aboard, Khalil ran to greet Carter with a salaam. Behind Carter was a curious man from the tower.

"Khalil," he asked, "where did you get this old crate?"

"My wives bought it at auction. Of course they had to use their brother as 'front man,' because they are women!" The man from the tower disappeared at a run, ready to satisfy the tower's curiosity.

"Danilya bin Zaid was our co-pilot today," Khalil said proudly. Danilya wore a dress which separated at the waist, so she could access the trousers beneath made of softer cloth—no one wanted cloth under foot while trying to fly. When they landed, she could close the skirt with a textured Velcro strip which appeared to be part of the design.

Danilya, they found during their visit, was a model for the younger women; she was the local version of Amelia Earhart; she had strut, and to state some of the young women lionized her would not be stretching the truth.

Her sister, Hanan, was a far lower key, reflective and creative. Hanan designed some of her sister's more modern pieces of clothes. She also designed a series of transparencies to show to visitors which might be put into a machine that projected them onto a white wall with singular clarity. She was always being creative about something.

When they spoke with each other about how best to proceed with the situation, Carter said "I think it would work best If we just relate to them as individuals."

"Fortunately, there seems to be a lot to relate to!" his wife answered.

It was at the end of their visit was when the miracle occurred.

C H A P T E R   2 6

Now July was slipping into the first weeks of August, and it was still school vacation. Mercy and her mother were in the garden, weeding, watering, and trimming. Jane passed by to see if Mercy wanted to play, but gardening was not her idea of fun, so she went on her way, waving to Carter as he backed out of the driveway. Valerie had been envisioning shifting shadows, yet could not make out the message; the danger was very great, she sensed, but not to anything she could relate it to.

As the sun was falling softly through the branches of the tree, throwing moving patterns on the grass where Valerie grew shade plants, she moved along towards it in the latter part of the morning, as it grew hotter. Mercy had found a special shovel for weeding, which she loved to use because it was so precise.

Her mother heard footsteps coming up the driveway, and she looked up to see a well-dressed man who tipped his hat to her.

"I was admiring your shade garden; I hope you don't mind my meandering up for a closer look," he explained.

"Please do," said Valerie, who assumed he would look at it from outside the garden fence. She was not in a mood for further conversation, for she was nearing the end of her tasks.

Suddenly she heard the garden fence gate latch open, as her daughter screamed, "Mommy!"

This time, the shadows had not coalesced into the shape of a man; this time, it was real.

Dropping her spade, she swung around to see the man trying to seize her daughter; he had no idea of the spiritual shield Khalil had once discerned around her, so while he could come within inches of her, he could not grasp her.

"What do you think you're doing?" Valerie screamed, as she leapt up behind him, bent her right arm around his neck, and seized her fist with her left hand, beginning to choke him as hard as she possibly could. He was asphyxiating slightly, but, was almost preternaturally strong. This automatically registered with Valerie as a signpost of the demonic. He shook her off, turned and pushed her backward so that she fell so swiftly it almost knocked the wind out of her, crying to Mercy, "Get King!"

King had his own ideas when he heard his name invoked and had no need of the Attack command as he jumped straight out onto the lawn.

She heard him beginning to utter a deep growl, so she knew help would be swift, but clearly in the short intervening time she was in trouble. He straddled her and seized her long hair, wound it around her neck, and began to choke her with it.

Then, with the inspiration born of desperation, she bit him; before he could pull his arm back, she grabbed him by the hair with both hands so he could not easily pull away. He moved his arm over to help to try to break her grasp, so Valerie let go her one hand, reaching backward as far as she could, feeling the texture of soil and mulch at the edge of the garden; possessing herself of a handful of it, she heard a yell as she threw it in his eyes, and bit deeper into his arm.

In two panther leaps, King had reached her, eyes glowering, and leapt onto the man's back, sinking his teeth into his neck, pulling him over backwards, then standing over him, growling, as Mercy told him, "If you move, he will tear your throat open!" The man's strength was somehow not equal to King's teeth. *The hound of Heaven.*

It was Mercy who dialled Carter's office from her mother's mobile and screamed, "Poppy, we need you!"

I hope I won't need a bridge for my front teeth, thought Valerie.

Carter rang Met. "John! Please send an unmarked team flying squad car to my house as quickly as possible!" He dropped a pile of papers he had gathered so carefully, which now scattered randomly over the floor.

He heard John punch an extension to command, "Get me a speed driver for Judge Braxton *immediately.*"

This was the scene which greeted Carter as he sprinted up the driveway: Mercy was lying beside her mother, who had blood from her nefarious guest running over the lower part of her face, and looked like a vampire. Bruising was also beginning to develop under her cheeks the clasp had fallen out of her hair, which was now tangled with mud, mulch, and grass, with King straddling the assailant, guarding him tightly.

Three bobbies from the local police station had run up the driveway. Ripping open the intruder's shirt revealed a five- pointed witches' star on his chest. Even three men had trouble subduing him once King let go, but finally, they wrapped the assailant in a strait jacket, put a coat over the jacket, and took him off to their police station

"Valerie!" he burst out, seeing blood on her face.

"I bit him," she replied.

"We'll get a doctor to give him a knock out shot," one of them said.

It won't do any good.

Then he turned to his little girl, asking, "Mercy, do you think you could get Mum a wet towel so we can clean her up a bit?" He managed to say this in a calm voice for Mercy's sake. Meanwhile he put her head on his lap, which ruined that pair of trousers. *Damn! What a time to have a pistol stored upstairs in a lock box! Thank God this chap wasn't armed. I must show Mercy how to open the lock box.*

"How did they know I left—that little bitch!" exclaimed Carter. Jane had seen him driving away from the house.

"Poppy! Please don't blame Jane!" Mercy stuttered. All the same, Carter had been right. Something had surely happened.

Carter sat with Valerie's head on his lap; taking the wet towel, he gently began to wipe her face. He was shaken and weak in the knees from shock. *It's over now, he told himself.* He had had plenty of opportunity to learn how to quell his fears. Mercy hesitantly came over.

"Don't worry about your friend," Carter told her.

Meanwhile, John had arrived, and Valerie was giving as clear an account as she could with a very sore jaw. *I hope I never have to bite anyone again!* It was decided to transport everyone to the fortress that night; Mohammed could tend Valerie; an xray showed a thin fracture line along her cheek, and the good doctor affixed Valerie's teeth in place properly and put plaster over them until they grew back into the gums without wiggling.

The questioners who had picked up Jane at a local playground were getting nowhere. Why had she told someone Carter was leaving the house? At last, Jane cracked—she had been terrified by her three- week separation from her mother during the trial, and somehow, the devil you do know is less frightening than the devil you don't know, and this fact had been used to bully her.

Threats of separation from her child—where the trail had easily led—and threats of years of jailtime only appeared to amuse Jane's mother. Finally they asked Valerie what to do.

"Separate Jane from her mother."

And so it was that the old adage that little pitchers have big ears was a true as ever. Jane had listened to meetings in her mother's living room crouched behind the top of the stairs. The night a witchcraft ceremony would take place, the field in Sussex, the 'super 'coven—Jane gave these all, with her only stipulation that no one ever tell her mother.

"If he hadn't spoken to me, I would have never even known he was there; he could have hopped the fence and come at me, for I had my back turned to him. I would have known nothing was wrong until Mercy called out."

"Does this mean now we will be targets?" The idea his wife and daughter might not be safe frightened him.

"Mercy is safe. It's that whatchamaycallit Khalil saw. As for me—do you remember how I told you about my attack in the Callahan tunnel?"

"Something to the effect you could not stop, or you would be overcome?"

"Yes, I am so sorry. It really is, though He slay me, yet will I trust him. Let me know if you want out."

"This is for better or worse, Valerie. I do not propose to ever leave you. I could have never married anyone more interesting than you are. Or one as dear."

"My love," she replied.

Valerie peeked in on Mercy after she was asleep at the fortress. She smiled, because Mercy had wiggled into bed with King, who always slept with his paws hanging over the bed so she could snuggle up against his back.

Carter's first sighting of his brother-in-law George in the flesh occurred when he arrived at their home by taxi, accompanied by two Oriental looking young men, for an overnight visit, on their way to a tour of England and Scotland. George had plans to vet a large shipbuilding facility in Glasgow.

He was slightly shorter than his elder brother Charlie, but shared his preference for fedora hats; he did not like the sun in his eyes and who could say he was wrong? He still did not wear glasses.

Generally he wore a Barbour all weather overcoat (with a liner in cold weather). He still was cadet-erect and walked with the measured step of one used to synchronized marching, while a faint whiff of the military still clung to him, betokening a lacking in the ordinary man. He wiped his feet on the doormat and removed his hat. Carter noticed that his movements had the rhythm of some inner clock.

Humorously, he referred to the nodding boys behind him. "They are always watching my back. I would like to introduce V□nh Tran Le and his elder brother, Vinh S□nh Tranan—otherwise known as Le and Tran. I am their legal guardian. Soon I may be able to adopt them."

Their presence added a new practice to the house for the evening. It was a Vietnamese custom to don their pyjamas, come down to the living room, and eat large Vietnamese cookies before bed. Mercy enjoyed this greatly, as well as having some young men visit. Her parents could not enter into the ritual with quite her childish enthusiasm.

When John Hawkins learned that George was a West Point graduate, had served in the Army Corps of Engineers, and was skilled in situational analysis and mapping terrain, he asked if George might like to aid in the search for the site in Surrey represented by a small map at the back of Mrs. Collins' notebook.

When Valerie rang, George gave a short 'yes.' They would return to London and book in at a hotel a few days earlier than they had planned to end their trip, in order to be present at the date for the meeting of the coven. Then, George would re-book their flight home, and they would fly back to Scotland to complete their trip. It was all arranged quickly and efficiently, with no blowback from the boys. They were adapted to George's swift ability to change plans. Indeed, upon hearing the word witchcraft, George appeared to share the Herrington family's training from Jack Tottle for eradicating it.

So it was, one morning, George was peering at the map in the back of Mrs. Collin's little book through a magnifying glass, trying to match it with a large-scale map beside it.

As they walked to the helicopter they had been assigned, George said, "That logo has to go if you want to do this covertly." For the sides were painted the legend, 'Metropolitan Police,' and George added, "Anyone who saw it might realize we're a bit odd to be flying over Sussex. We need some spray paint—it covers large jobs and dries quickly. You can use the Herrington logo!" He said with a laugh. *Too bad Sis isn't here!*

The next day he appeared changed into rough corduroy pants and his old combat boots—which everyone who had been in service claimed were the most comfortable of all footwear— and which went everywhere with him. A bag held several sandwiches, and a canteen was filled with water. "I'd recce this area," he said, finally. Their pilot was skilled at contour chasing (hugging the landscape). John appeared a bit bilious at the gills as they brushed close to the treetops. George noticed that John was looking a trifle green. *Give the poor bloke something to do.*

"I'd get your camera ready after we pass this next stand of trees," he told John, as he wrote out the area coordinates." No—probably the next one," he said, as they dropped down for a look. He was right. It was the next one. The pilot dropped down below the tree line again, causing John to throw up slightly.

"Is that it?" John asked.

"Yes—look at that altar." George was sketching the venue. True to form, George had found the small field secluded from the rest of the landscape by trees.

Upon return, John began to formalize his plans, drawing on members of his force he deemed ready for the task.

All the next day long, the sky had darkened.

By nightfall, a light rainfall began.

John had planned his operation meticulously. Everyone was in place before the coven participants arrived, so there would be no stumbling or other noise-making in the woods, while cars had been driven off further down the road. Each man wore ear plugs, connected to John's microphone. The ceremony was, as reported, to be in an open field surrounded by trees, as oblivious as possible from any roads or houses.

The evening became blanketed with humidity, while in the very distance was a faint rumble of thunder, and a gradually heavier scent of ozone began to drift through the air. The Sidi was part of the ground crew, and asked John if Khalil cold accompany him. At the last minute, Khalil asked John if he would grant him the favor of accompanying him as weapon bearer, since John would be guiding the insertion into the trees from his microphone. This approach proved to be humble enough that John said yes, for Valerie had mentioned what a good shot he was—the best in Sidi's team. Khalil rarely had to aim for body mass; he was too good a shot.

They heard people entering the field, yet stayed hidden; there could be no arrests until there was something to arrest them for.

As John and Khalil moved closer, their movement covered by the noise in the field, first, they smelt the smoke; then they were startled as a few crackles of fire emerged above the tree tops. The fire had been doused with an accelerant.

John now knew it was urgent to send a scout forward; he tapped Khalil on the shoulder and motioned him to move in. Creeping along the ground, utilizing leaves and branches for cover and silent movement, Khalil, barefooted, moved swiftly toward the noise. He picked a spot between two trees tightly standing together from which to see. He used the notch to stabilize his rifle. A pyre of wood was burning ferociously; a pregnant mother, doped and tied up with rope lay in front of the altar, and a figure in a black cape and hood stood in front of her, holding a scimitar. The rest of the participants were sky clad.

Khalil suffered no hesitation in the following action. *He is going to kill the mother and take the child.* The wizard began to raise his sword, held vertically, point down. He had brought it up his chest, and halted for a few seconds to gather himself before the downward plunge; Khalil shot him in the forehead. He fell backwards.

"Move in! Move in!" Khalil shouted to John. Suddenly the woods began brimming with moving personnel.

The moon was now a ghostly galleon, tossed by gigantic waves which curled over the top of one other, one wave disappearing only to re-appear again, which no earthly vessel could have withstood; fringes of foam topped the waves. The thunder sounded directly overhead.

"Stand back!" Khalil cried. "Stand!" John shouted into his microphone. Heavy lightning began to hit. Large bolts of electricity running through the soil formed into balls of St. Elmo's fire which rolled across the ground, dropping members of the coven, stunned, uttering horrible shrieks of terror that no one who ever heard them that night would ever forget.

Khalil staggered toward John, having absorbed some electric shock himself. Then he succumbed, falling at John's feet, muttering, "Call Mohammed."

Mohammed threw a rubber mat over Khalil and the immediate ground around him so he could approach him safely. Immediately he listened to his heart. "A little adrenalin to steady the heart beat," he told his friend. He checked his vital signs, and told him to lie still until they could bring in a stretcher to carry him out and take him to a hospital.

"But I could get up," Khalil protested weakly.

"You shouldn't. Don't be a hero,'" said Mohammed.

"I am sorry I fired before your order. I was afraid of how fast that man was moving," Khalil told John.

"Jolly good you did, or she'd be dead," said John.

The only note of what had happened that night was in the weather report: 'unusually heavy thunder and outpourings of lightning' in the Sussex area.

The storm rumbled on its way so paramedics could tend the participants lying all over the ground. All the participants were charged as accomplices.

No one could really understand the motivation for what had just happened except Valerie. She encapsulated the situation.

"The devil found a gullible megalomaniac who believed a story of reversing the world religion through a satanic ceremony, one which would reverse the sacrifice Abraham never made, a world which they would then rule. That is why they had absolutely no fear of incarceration. Remember that the devil prowls about the earth like a lion seeking souls he may devour."

I only try earthly law, thought her husband.

C H A P T E R   2 8

The call came through at 3 a.m., London time.

"Sis?"

Buddy?"

"Who is it?"

"Pop."

By now Carter was out of bed and halfway down the stairs to enable him to pick up the downstairs telephone.

"Carter?"

"Present, Buddy."

"It's congestive heart failure. No one really knows how fast or slow it's gonna be."

Now they heard King begin to prowl, for he knew that something was afoot.

Buddy continued, "I don't know how long we'll be here. They tried to stick an IV into Pop and he said he was not going to listen to that beep, beep,beep, so the nurse told him that after a while, he'd get used to it and go to sleep.

"He sat up, looked her in the eye with that stare of his, and said, "Like Hell I will. Call the doctor." Of course he knows all the doctors on a long term basis, so he told Patrick when he hustled on up he was not going to leave this earth hearing beep, beep, and if they couldn't turn it off, he was leaving."

"We have to sign you out," Patrick said, and Pop was kinda insulted.

Pop said, "We've been friends for thirty years. If you want to pick this particular moment to be a pain in the ass, never trust a man who turns into a jackal when the wolf is down. I've got everything at home I need at home, or Karen can get it."

Carter interspersed, "I do not know American law that well, but I know patients can refuse treatments such as blood transfusions."

Relief flooded Valerie as he heard her husband's calm voice as he continued. "Buddy," Carter continued, "call Lt. Pearson."

Buddy used his cellphone to call Billy.

"Do I understand you are recommending law officers?" Patrick shouted at the telephone.

"I am. I'm a judge. I've seen every delaying tactic there is."

"Tell Pop he'd better be there when we arrive," said Valerie, through tears.

After several minutes, Buddy reported back. "I told Billy we were having trouble getting Pop out of the hospital."

"The one he helped build?" Billy had asked.

"The very one."

"I'm a hundred miles away. I'll be there fast as possible." Billy liked nothing better than a good reason to step on the gas.

News of Roulon's failing health spread across northwest counties like a benumbing fog. So was his request for no visitors, as it would only tire him. Billy called his major at Ranger barracks, who told him to go to the ranch and park his car sideways across the gate.

"Use a horse to patrol the perimeter so there won't be any fence crashers."

In England, Carter phoned and managed to reserve three tickets on the early morning flight from Heathrow.

"Should we really take Mercy?" Valerie asked.

"I wanna go!"

Carter was methodically packing his suitcase. "I think we should," he replied. "Come along, Mercy, I'll help you pack." It was the first time he had insisted on something for Mercy, overriding Valerie's objections.

It would be a problem finding transport to the airport at 4:30 in the morning, without a reservation for a car. With a bolt of inspiration, Carter called the night desk of the Metropolitan police. John had given them a name and number if he needed aid at night. Blessed Met2 sent a squad car with a siren (if needed). Someone from the canine patrol was with them to care for King.

Valerie was tearfully packing while Carter opened his office safe for the passports. At times Valerie found Carter too methodical, but this particular morning she appreciated it.

Safely on the flight, Carter advised Valerie to take one of her sleeping pills. "What about Mercy?" she asked.

Mercy was wide awake with excitement, and Carter wanted to make a few more phone calls en route. So the two of them stayed wide awake.

A collective of Herringtons—Claudia, George, Le and Tran—waited for Diego in New York. They were a bereft little bunch, huddled together in a light rain. They had decided to wait for the arrival of Valerie's flight, since if Diego had to make two flights to New York, it made no sense. Only Carter, when newly arrived, had an umbrella.

They all knew Roulon would die "someday" but that "someday" was always future. Now it had arrived: Le and Tran were very nervous, as they had never met the family before, or been to Christian funeral. They did not want to embarrass Mr. George.

The family had heard that George had adopted two Vietnamese boys, but thought little about it, (except for Claudia) as it did not seem likely they would ever meet.

In Texas, people came quietly to the fence. They respected Roulon's request for no visitors, but left items there in tribute. A Native American tribal chief bearing a decorated staff left a special blanket and a note asking them to put the blanket near Roulon. Jack Tottle arrived to simply sit in a rocking chair at the other end of the porch, should Roulon need him.

Carter rang the Sidi in London, for he knew his friend would be offended to not have been kept abreast of such major family news. So it was that Karen answered a call in Texas, to hear a familiar voice.

"Pop, would you like to speak to Sidi?" She held the receiver for him.

"Darned straight I would! Where are you?"

"At the Hague. Kahlil rang me."

"Could you boys possibly get out here? I'm gonna need some strong pallbearers."

Everyone on the porch could hear the Sidi's loud answer, a voice he used when speaking on the telephone through often dicey connections. "I would be honored. Do not worry. We will land on your back runway."

CHAPTER 29

"Mercy, dear, let go. I must use the loo," instructed her Poppy.

Reclaiming his seat, like many an adult charged with tending a hyper -activated, excited child, he was beginning to tire. Also he had a deep desire to be with his wife for a moment or two, when George intervened, asking Mercy if she would want to play with Le and Tran; they had a pack of cards.

Carter moved up a row to where Valerie had found room to stretch out over three seats to sleep. Sliding under her head he placed it on his lap, and automatically, although still asleep, a hand reached out to hold his. When Valerie woke, Carter kept holding her hand.

He put his head in the small angle between the wall and the window, and dozed off. He awoke to hear the bump, bump of landing gear.

Upon deplaning, they had a surprise: they were escorted through customs. George often watched debates at the United Nations and had friends there, one of whom had arranged this bypass for him.

They were now seated on their own Gulfstream with Diego piloting. Claudia was sitting by the window seat with her coat wrapped around her, but still was shivering, so George sat down next to her.

"You never came home after the war."

"No, sister-in-law dear, I did not."

"Something is not being said here, George. I suspect it's Charlie?"

"Right, Claudia. He has always been competitive with me. I had a touch of PTSD and I was vulnerable."

"Now he has the responsibility and he knows you have a good set of brains, no matter his prejudices."

"Yes, but he has Buddy, who definitely should run the ranch. Charlie's been in oil too long, he's lost the touch."

George appreciated Claudia's candor.

They were beginning the descent to the ranch. By now they were all dead tired, running on artificial energy. On the other side of the sound barrier, Karen, Buddy, BJ, Jessica, Stella, and Charlie were waiting.

Roulon was lounging in the chaise longue provided for him from which he could see and hear all the familiar sounds of the environment he loved so much.

When Charlie had arrived, he had come up on the porch to ask, "Dad, shall I…" His father held up his hand.

"Your decision, son, you have power of attorney." Charlie cringed inwardly to feel the weight now on his shoulders. Seeing George, he said bullishly, "I see the prodigal son has returned."

George simply walked around him and mounted the porch stairs, approached his father, clapped his heels together and rendered a smart salute.

"Sit down, Major! What the hell took you so long?" *So he followed my promotions.*

"Well Pop, you remember when you came home, you were heroes. We were baby killers."

"Yeah, I know, son. What about these boys I hear you have?"

"Ah. I killed their grandfather. He was alone in the open. Truly, Pop, he was too old to be a soldier, but I could not really tell until I was able to draw closer. I thought he might be a decoy. I had to get him to fire first under the rules of engagement, of course, but thankfully he was a lousy shot. He had papers on him, so I took them; one had a home address."

"Sounds like you did all the right things."

"Thanks, Pop. But he didn't see me—there was another option.'"

"Not in wartime thinking, son." Roulon touched George's sleeve. "'No more time to turn aside and brood upon life's bitter mysteries.'" (Valerie was not the only family member to like Yeats.) "No kids or your own, right? I'd remember."

George had been widowered. "Frances and I decided no on it. We heard a lot of tales about what Agent Orange did to foetuses. It's rather nice the boys refer to her as Mrs. George."

"You went back for them?"

"I wrote ahead to get an OK. The grandmother appreciated the offer of an education in the States."

"Got them with you?"

"Of course."

I'd like to meet them."

George called out in an unfamiliar language. Le and Tran approached slowly; somewhat intimidated, they put their hands together and bowed multiple times. Roulon held out his hand. The boys looked questioningly at Mr. George, who nodded.

George noticed his father had leaned forward slightly to shake hands; after he had finished, he slumped back.

"Come along, boys, it's time to settle in."

Now the signal from the hangar went off to indicate an incoming aircraft. Charlie picked up a house intercom and ordered, "turn on the floodlights on the airstrip."

Buddy, at that moment, had one of those strange infusions of wisdom, when he realized that the ordinary had morphed into the extraordinary: his father seemed to have one last plan.

C H A P T E R   3 0

Carter raced over the sound barrier with Mercy hot on his tail. He salaamed Sidi, but hugged Khalil, who reciprocated.

Mercy cried, "Hello, old goat!" and received the ritual reply, "Hello, little one!"

"I'm ten now! But I'm sad about grandpa!"

Sidi sensed a coming storm when she asked, "Why has God allowed so many people in my life to die? Why do we have to die, anyway?"

Once again Carter caught an onrushing child, this time, one in tears.

I don't think original sin is going to cut it.

"Mercy, dear, you know how some of your clothes wear out, don't you?"

Sniffle, "Yes."

"That is what happens to our bodies."

"But that isn't what happened to Daddy!"

"No, it isn't. Mercy. Sometimes God overrides our natural span of years for His own reasons, or an illness which is able to override nature, seizes on us; our natural Biblical lifespan is threescore and ten—seventy. Many people live beyond that. All this is clothed in mystery—we do not understand everything, nor are we meant to. "Perplexed but not driven to despair," as your mother's favorite Bible verse goes—"not driven to despair," when almost anyone would have been." *Yes, she did say once if she'd been driven all the way to despair she might have killed herself, but somehow, it stopped just short of that. That's too harsh for a child.*

"Poppy—is that why you have some grey hairs? Is your hair wearing out? Oh, Poppy—are you going to die?"

"Eventually, Mercy, but not now. Only when you've grown up."

"But I don't know what I want to be when I grow up!"

"Only a small percentage of the people know what they want to be when they grow up."

"You knew, didn't you?"

"I look upon that as a special kind of blessing. "Come on, let's see if your grandfather is awake."

"Do you think Jesus knew? After all he was sitting in the temple when he was twelve answering questions!" He took her hand. *This one's too deep for me—off to find Valerie or Jack.*

Valerie was sitting on the porch floor hugging her knees next to Jack. She was feeling semi-paralyzed with no idea what to do. *Didn't someone say the universe cracked and I fell out?* Now the structure of her former life was being completely destroyed.

Carter sat down on the floor beside her, unsure of what to say, until he muttered, "Call Pendragon before it's too late," for there was a big time difference. Off she went. Mercy stood tentatively behind him, waiting. Then something unusual happened. Roulon called her name.

"Go ahead," said Carter. Hesitantly, she walked over to her grandfather.

"I hear you are a bit of a scholar, "he said. "Could you read me a Psalm?"

"I guess so, Grandpa. Which one did you want?"

"Psalm 139." He pointed to a Bible on a table beside him. Mercy leafed through slowly. "Ah, here it is!" she exclaimed.

"First read it to me in Hebrew!"

His grand daughter complied.

'Where can I go from your Spirit?

Where can I flee from your presence?

If I say, "Surely the darkness will hide me

And the light become night around me
Even the darkness is not dark to you.
The night will shine like day
For darkness is as light to you.'"

Roulon lay back reflectively. "It sure will be nice to go somewhere where there is no night," he said.

"Don't you like stars, grandpa?"

"You ask Jack. God existed before He created earthly light. Earthly light and darkness do not exist in eternity. Sure, I believe I'm in for a new landscape. Tell you what. Ask your mother to come over here with us."

Mercy obediently scuffed her way off to Valerie.

"Mom, grandpa would like to see you." Valerie had been on the telephone and just hung up.

"Jack, I don't know what to do to help her," said Carter.

"Then get out of the way for someone who can."

"Who is…?"

"Don't try to run in front of the Holy Spirit."

"So you're in the dark?"

"Often!" said Jack.

As Valerie approached her father and sat down, he asked, "Play me a song, daughter?"

"Do you have one in mind?"

"Green Pastures." Sending Mercy to find her aunt Jessica, she waited, holding his hand. Jessica returned with Mercy, handing Valerie a guitar.

"It's been a while, Pop."

"Yup."

'Going up yonder, to live in green pastures,
Where we will live and die nevermore,
Even the Lord will be in that number
When we have reached that heavenly shore.'

Valerie's voice was still clear from singing in church, but her fingering was sloppy; she didn't think her father even noticed, as he leaned back and closed his eyes.

"I've never heard her play the guitar," Carter remarked to Jack at their end of the porch.

"More's the pity."

Meanwhile, Stella saw the Sidi, and ran to him carrying a folder. No matter how tired the Sidi, she had a need to demonstrate her newly acquired skills, and handed him her photographic resumé notebook. He carefully flipped over each page, slowing down near the end.

At the gate, a dust- covered Ford truck pulled to a halt and a young man rolled down the window to talk to Billy Pearson, who moved his car out of the way to let him through.

"Oh, here comes Bobby—my boyfriend! Come and meet him!"

Stella must have coached him, for he did not endeavor to shake hands, but made a short bow.

"I am honored to meet you, sir."

"Ditto, young man." The Sidi continued flipping through the last pages of Stella's presentation. "These last are the same rock formation?"

"Yes, taken an hour apart from each other over twenty-four hours," said Bobby proudly. "I spent two days scouting Paolo Duro for the best rock formation. Then Stella spent twenty-four hours snapping. You get some very unusual shots at night. A friend put some of them in his shop window."

"These were not taken with my old Polaroid!"

"Mum and Poppy gave me this one for Christmas."

The Sidi surveyed Bobby. Faded jeans, plaid cotton shirt, belt and belt buckle, Stetson atop blond hair, boots. Nothing to indicate he aspired to something different.

"Bobby is a geologist," said Stella proudly.

"And what do you do out here?"

"Measure rock depths with a sweep, find good spots for aquafiers, know where rock formations run underground, and with the coming technology, do some work with shale and fracking. My last job was for an up and coming quarry; they wanted to find a deposit of igneous rock near the alluvial rock they were using for cement.

Now I have one in Nevada finding playas and trying to decide whether they are over deposits of lithium brine beneath them."

C H A P T E R 3 1

Now there was one thing Roulon distinctively disliked about funerals. "No viewing, I don't want my mouth sewed shut." But a yes for blood letting. "I don't want to wake up underground." Also he thought the line of black Cadillacs was pretentious and probably the only time many folk get to ride in a Cadillac.

"I'd like to be pulled one last time by horse and wagon. Bring me the phone. Skat." This translated that he wished to make a private call.

Valerie and Buddy went to the stables to see the wagon and harness were in shape. "I can barely move," she told her brother. "I feel paralyzed."

When they returned to the porch, Karen said, "He's going fast now—I'd like to get him some oxygen." But Roulon didn't want it even though his breathing was considerably labored. That evening, he stared out at the sky in a way which made his children feel he knew he was looking at his last sunset. Karen had given him a number for the local rabbi. It was his last phone call. His last word was to Karen, as she wheeled him along: he pulled on her sleeve. "Mabel?"

"She's all right, Pop. Tonight is the High Chapparal."

His children decided to stay in the stone room with him, so they could sing hymns, unaccompanied by instruments. Carter and Claudia and Karen, Le and Tran (who managed to wedge in on each side of Jessica) Stella and Mercy sat with Mabel, who was watching her favorite television show. When it finished, she went to bed, while Sidi, Khalil and Jack enjoyed sitting outside in the warm night air. A quarter of an hour later, Roulon was gone.

He was delivered by hearse to the funeral home about 10 p.m. George and Buddy were with him as his life blood ran out into a drain in the floor. The undertaker had washed the body and placed it in a simple shroud. As to the question what clothing did they wish to have put on him, Valerie offered the thought they should simply wrap him in the beautiful blanket presented by the local tribe. He was placed in a simple casket his workers had knocked together.

"That's good," said Buddy. "The less the better. Pop didn't want to go toxic." No, Pop did not like clothing not made of natural fiber or embalming fluid. He was transferred back to the house by hearse, where the casket was lifted out and placed on the wagon. They seemed to sense the solemnity of the occasion. Buddy jumped into the wagon seat and took the reins.

"Put her up here, Carter." Mercy was lifted up beside her uncle.

None of them made a move to change their clothes. The rabbi and cantor arrived, and seeing the horses and wagon, were pleased to see Roulon would be buried before midnight on the day he had died, which was also a custom the Sidi and Khalil adhered to.

As if to light their way, the stars were shining brightly over the naked landscape, making shadows of the taller plants, and footing quite precise. So, about a hundred yards from the grave, they all stopped, deciding to carry it the last part of the way, and removed the casket from the wagon. They lined up with Charlie and George in front, the rabbi and the cantor in the middle, and Sidi and Khalil at the rear.

"Fellas, we're going to have to march in cadence or we'll have a disaster," said George.

"Well, you do it, Mr. West Point," said Charlie.

The women were standing beside the casket, watching it lifted onto six shoulders. Claudia took her husband's arm and shook it.

"This is not the time, Charlie, grow up." Small though she was, her effect was large.

Charlie glanced at her. "Sorry," he said. George glanced at her sideways.

"I'm going to give Pop the real thing," said George. "I hadda good home but I left, left—left, right left right…"

Arriving at the gravesite, the women stretched ropes on the ground before the casket was laid down on top of them. Everyone was able to hold onto a piece of it as they lowered him down into a grave which he had typically ordered dug three days before. Sidi noticed that young Bobby appeared and stood behind Stella, then held her hand on the way home. *Appearances to the contrary, he understands that young woman needs gentle handling.*

Before this last obloquy, Jack stepped to the head of the casket. "You all know I use the verse Fr. Juan gave me," he remarked. "The souls of the just are in God's hand, and the torment shall no touch them. In the eyes of foolish men they seemed to be dead; their departure was reckoned as defeat, and their going from us a disaster. But they are at peace. For though in the sight of men they may be punished, they have a sure hope of immortality; after little chastisement they will receive great blessings, because the Lord has tested them and found them worthy to be his…those who have put their trust in him shall understand that he is true; the faithful shall attend him in love; for they are his chosen, and grace and mercy shall be theirs.'"

When he had finished, he moved to one side, and said, "Gentlemen." Sidi and the rabbi joined him. Sidi said a blessing in Arabic, and the rabbi pronounced the verse a faithful Jew was last supposed to hear: "Hear, O Israel, the Lord Thy God is one."

There was no eulogy. Roulon's opinion was, "If y'all don't know me by now it's too damn late." Suddenly Carter recognized his father in-law's plan: he died a child of Abraham—the first one to do so. He looked over at the Sidi, who smiled.

As they walked back to the house, George dropped back beside Jack. "That is the verse the priest to read at Frances's funeral. She was a Catholic." He reached into his pocket and pulled out a worn -out rosary. "She told me to carry it."

"Do you say it?"

"Mainly I just carry it."

"Are you all right?" Carter asked George, who was looking worn out.

"Got a checkup appointment at Sloan Kettering when we get home. Don't mention it to Sis."

Mercy was definitely dragging, and Buddy had already driven away, so Carter tried something he'd seen men do: he lifted her up on his shoulders. "Come on, small fry," he said, using a family epithet. As she slumped into sleep, he held onto her wrists.

Back at the house, the rabbi and the cantor departed, as did Jack and Bobby; the Sidi and Khalil went over to the guest house, and the quiet of finitude settled over the house, emptying it of feeling; hollowed out, exhaled of life, uncannily still. Slowly the rest of the family went to bed.

George said to Le and Tran, "I know you boys didn't get to ask him this yourself, but my father approved the idea of changing your last name to Herrington, now that you are adopted. He had some legal papers drawn up."

Le and Tran rejoiced.

Jack Tottle had been right. Working with her brothers to make her father's funeral come out just the way he wanted it had somehow lifted Valerie's spirits, and her determination to strengthen the things that remained.

Before leaving Texas, the siblings decided to have a preliminary sort of meeting in the stone room—only the four of them, it was understood.

Charlie had plunged ahead simply because he was the eldest, although there was no primogeniture in the Herrington family. His first item of business was one that seemed important to him.

"I suppose, George, you'll be wanting to come back and pick up part of the action."

His brother replied, "No indeed, brother dear. You take the high road and I'll take the low road—why don't we just keep it that way. I've got things to do. I'll submit my yearly at our meeting as usual."

To Valerie, this declaration had the effect of a suddenly flattened tire, to wit, the impression Charlie had always had that he was standing guard on an *idée fixé* —a golden egg which he always assumed George would attempt to pull out from under him. *Of course, she thought, this is only an unconscious recognition that George is the smarter of the two of them, and Charlie knew everyone always knew it.*

Charlie looked over anxiously at Claudia, and George elicited she had indeed had words to share with Charlie on the subject of George.

Carter had always felt Valerie had a bit of split personality— here in Texas with family, she was more relaxed, funnier, more 'at home.' As they flew out over the Atlantic, these tendencies began to slowly vanish and another personality appeared—her English formality.

CHAPTER 32

High Court was still in summer recess. Carter realized Valerie had become anxious about when her daughter-in-law would go into labor. While she usually left her mobile phone scattered around the house—and they had to ring it on the house phone or Carter's mobile to find it—she now kept it close by. He suggested they go to Pendragon for a few days.

They put their luggage in the Rover. Mercy, surprisingly, wanted to stay at home. She would miss some of her usual things to do; as well, there were no children her age to play with at Pendragon.

On arrival, Carter had the ritual of entering by the front door; he just had to make sure that marvellous staircase was still there, and no one had taken to any renovating project which might have wiped it out. He hoped that it would remain the same during the duration of his lifetime. Yet in a house of renovators, he always had to check. Then he and Valerie fell victim to the soporific country air; after a nap, they nibbled on some tea sandwiches: Carter indulged in his favorite, egg salad.

There was a hustle and bustle in the house that proclaimed this was not an average day. The foreman had come over to confer with Adry about an order they needed to prepare for Monday. "Could you just over and calculate the fall for us, boss?"

"What is happening?"

"Oh, Adry is taking down a tree."

"That definitely is something I would like to see," Brie exclaimed, receiving a veto from her husband as she was about to give birth any day now. Her husband mentioned that a fall was always a bit dodgy and he wanted to take no chances.

Valerie declined to come to watch the fall—it would be a few years before Carter knew why.

Arriving at the condemned tree, Adry asked, "What are the stats?" The foreman showed diameter, height, and estimated weight, then plotted a fall that would not damage other trees. Adry sat down to make his calculations. "O.K.," he said after a while of consulting his slide rule, "Let's loop her, John," which meant attaching special long rope to the top of the tree so they had some control over the fall.

John wiggled into his harness. He had been very indignant over having to wear it, as he had never had an accident.

"I know that and you know that, John, but the business insurance company does not. New rules. If we don't comply, we can't insure the business."

As John climbed higher, the coil of rope connected to the harness played out, while a special winch on the ground kept on turning, absorbing the extra play of rope. It would lock in place, then lower the climber down. John cheerily climbed to the top of the tree, wiring the branches at the top, then throwing the remainders of the wires down to the ground crew.

"OK," said Adry, "cut in from this angle. Get down here, John." The ground crew used the winch to lower John to the ground. Men kept pulling on the rope rig John had looped with heavy gloves on their hands, because the tree had already begun its slow topple. As it neared its angle of pitch, Adry shouted, "Go! Go! Go!"

The men dropped the wires, running way from the spot. Moments after, the whole tree began to fall slowly, then more swiftly, landing at approximately just where everyone had wished, without damaging any of the other trees. "Good fall, boss!" "John shouted.

There was champagne for dinner, which Brie watched plaintively. Adry moved his glass over towards her and she stuck her forefinger into Adry's glass, then put it in her mouth and sucked off the residue.

After dinner she began to have pains, so most of the company sat up to find out if it was real or false labor, except for Carter, who, being a pragmatist, went to bed. Although he was in a deep sleep, someone was shaking him.

"Lemee alone," he muttered.

"Carter, its' time!"

"Time?"

"Brie and Adry are getting ready to leave for the hospital."

"Ohhh."

"Go back to sleep. I can ride with them."

Like hell you can. I'm not about to pull another St. Francis.

"Give me five minutes!" he said, and, as he had been lying in bed with his clothes on. He seemed to be ready, but then she saw him disappear into the bathroom.

"What are you doing?"

"I am shaving. I don't want to be a yobo on this occasion."

She heard the hum of an electric razor signal that he was in a hurry.

Only Carter would think of that.

Carter carefully followed the dirt road leading to the main road, one that was paved, and picked up so much speed Valerie was frightened.

"Relax," he instructed. "My defence skills included fast driving. I'll catch Adry and we will follow them." So it was they were all able to walk into the hospital together.

As they exited the Rover, she asked Carter to hold her arm. "I've been hyperventilating," she said, after taking a few woozy steps.

Adry registered while the nurses whisked Brie away to prepare her for childbirth—*shave her pubic hair and get her into a hospital gown*-Valerie began to breathe more deeply.

"We'll put her in a comfortable room until she is fully dilated and ready for the O.R."

"She is so fragile! I'm afraid she may have to have a Caesarean!"

"Don't kid yourself. That little body is 100% muscle."

The elevator stopped at lobby and Adry stepped out. "It will probably be a while. She would like some company."

They sat on a bench right outside the door to her room, hearing her struggle with each contraction; but in between, Brie was watching a local soccer game on television; as there was one in the lobby, they were able to watch together, mixing exclamations with grunts.

Now it was time to go into the O.R, and the nurses were covering them all in green gowns and caps. There seemed to be no assumption anyone would stay behind. Births such as these were celebratory occasions, sometimes attended by members of the staff; the mothers were far too busy to be shy! Later Brie said she would not have minded at that point if the whole village were there.

He was standing at the door, when a nurse asked, did he not want to co"I am only her step father."

The nurse understood without a word being said, and spread a blanket over Brie's mid-section. She led Carter to Brie's head, and left him there. Her feet were in stirrups.

"Push!" said the doctor, for Brie had been panting, awaiting instruction. She sucked in great breaths and pushed so hard her face turned red as she grunted or yelled loudly, with Adry cheering her on.

"Raise me up a bit!" she said to Adry. He put one arm under her left shoulder and signaled Carter to take his hand from the other side.

"Now, lift gently!"

"What are you doing?" asked the doctor.

"It's a better position than lying flat for her," said Adry.

The cardinal rule of childbirth, in certain societies, is that the mother is always right. Carter began to feel his arm shake with effort. *This is absolutely somewhere I have never been—I had no idea what birth was like. Adry was right. She may be little, but she is very strong.*

"I see the head. It's crowning," proclaimed the doctor. "Give us a few good more strong pushes, Brie! "He held his arms under her, ready to catch something. "Here it comes!"

A cry—life! "It's a boy!" The doctor cut and tied the umbilical cord, then something floppy and gooey dropped out. Good Lord! Was she all right?

"It's just the placenta," said Valerie. A nurse pulled a waste basket over to receive it.

Now Brie was wheeled into the recovery room, where she would stay until her natural elimination processes were working again. She was surprised that the mothers who had been anaesthetized did not know their babies had been born, and kept popping up to ask the nurses the same questions over and over.

But, on the night of Hew's birth, back at the house, the family all had a surge of exultation which made sleep impossible. Caught in the wave of such creative impulse, Carter found himself at the kitchen table, picked up a pen, and began to write.